RAYMOND CHANDLER'S PHILIP MARLOWE

THE LITTLE SISTER

RAYMOND CHANDLER'S PHILIP MARLOWE

THE LITTLE SISTER

Adapted and Illustrated by
MICHAEL LARK

Lettered by
WILLIE SCHUBERT

Colored by
ALEX WALD

Cover Art by
STERANKO

Art Director
DEAN MOTTER

A Byron Preiss Book

A Fireside Book
Simon & Schuster Editions

Published by Simon & Schuster

FIRESIDE
Rockefeller Center
1230 Avenue of the Americas
New York, NY 10020

A limited edition of this book was previously published in 1995, with a limitation of 110 copies.

FIRESIDE and colophon are registered trademarks of Simon & Schuster Inc.

Designed by Dean Motter

Manufactured in the United States of America

10 9 8 7 6 5 4 3 2 1

Library of Congress Cataloging-in-Publication Data

Raymond Chandler's Philip Marlowe: *The Little Sister*.
p. cm.
A full-color graphic format of the detective story.
"A Fireside book."
ISBN 0-684-82933-9
I. Chandler, Raymond, 1888-1959. Little sister.
PN6727.R33 1997
813' .52—dc20
96-42005 CIP

Executive Editor Byron Preiss
Editor Dean Motter
Associate Editor Ken Grobe
Contributing Editor Howard Zimmerman

RAYMOND CHANDLER, one of the twentieth century's most admired authors, was born in Chicago in 1888 and educated at Dulwich College, England. He worked at various times as poet, teacher, book reviewer, and accountant. During World War I he served in the R.A.F. In 1919 he returned to the United States where he became director for a number of independent oil companies. After the Great Depression put an end to his business he turned to writing. The first of his stories appeared in *Black Mask* magazine. His first Philip Marlowe novel, *The Big Sleep*, was published in 1939. It was followed by *Farewell, My Lovely*, *The High Window*, *The Lady in the Lake*, *The Little Sister*, *The Long Goodbye*, and *Playback*. Raymond Chandler lived most of the last decades of his life in Southern California. He died in 1959.

MARLOWE

The pulp magazine detective stories of the '30s that spawned hard-boiled crime fiction were direct descendants of the dime novels of the old west. They had much more to do with the exploits of Doc Holiday and Bat Masterson than with the British Penny Dreadfuls featuring Sherlock Holmes, Bulldog Drummond and their peers.

It is no surprise then that Los Angeles continues to be the favorite locale for that genre of fiction. It was carved from the "wild west"—through "six-gun justice."

This was Philip Marlowe's heritage.

Marlowe was essentially a cowboy. A rugged, solitary—and to all outwardly appearances, amoral—individual. These kinds of personalities emerged quite readily from the West. If the Gold Rush didn't produce them, the migrations to Hollywood and Las Vegas did. Brutality was really a question of survival—not a cultural trait.

In contrast, the felons of the East were disenfranchised souls baked in the crucible of industrial expansion and urban decay.

Certainly cruelty, greed, hopelessness, and despair were common enough throughout the country in the early part of the century. But even in post-war America, Los Angeles was a frontier town. And New York was *still* a European city. Los Angeles was to the West what the Old World had been to Boston and New Amsterdam two hundred years earlier.

Sunset Boulevard really has more in common with the streets of Laredo than the Great White Way. Hollywood Hills is closer in spirit to the OK Corral than to the Bowery.

For all intents and purposes we're still living in Tombstone.

Chandler reminds us of that.

Dean Motter
Last seen in
an abandonded
warehouse on the
outskirts of town

BERCY

STEIN...

...WE HAVE TO TALK.

YEAH, LET'S TALK, YOU AND ME. ABOUT WEEPY MOYER.
WHERE IS--

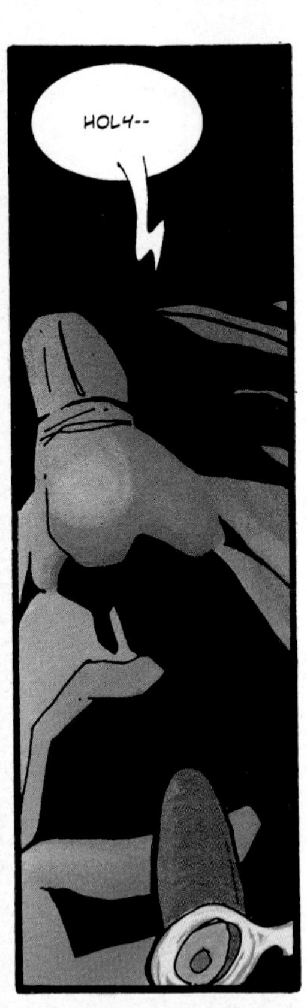
HOLY--

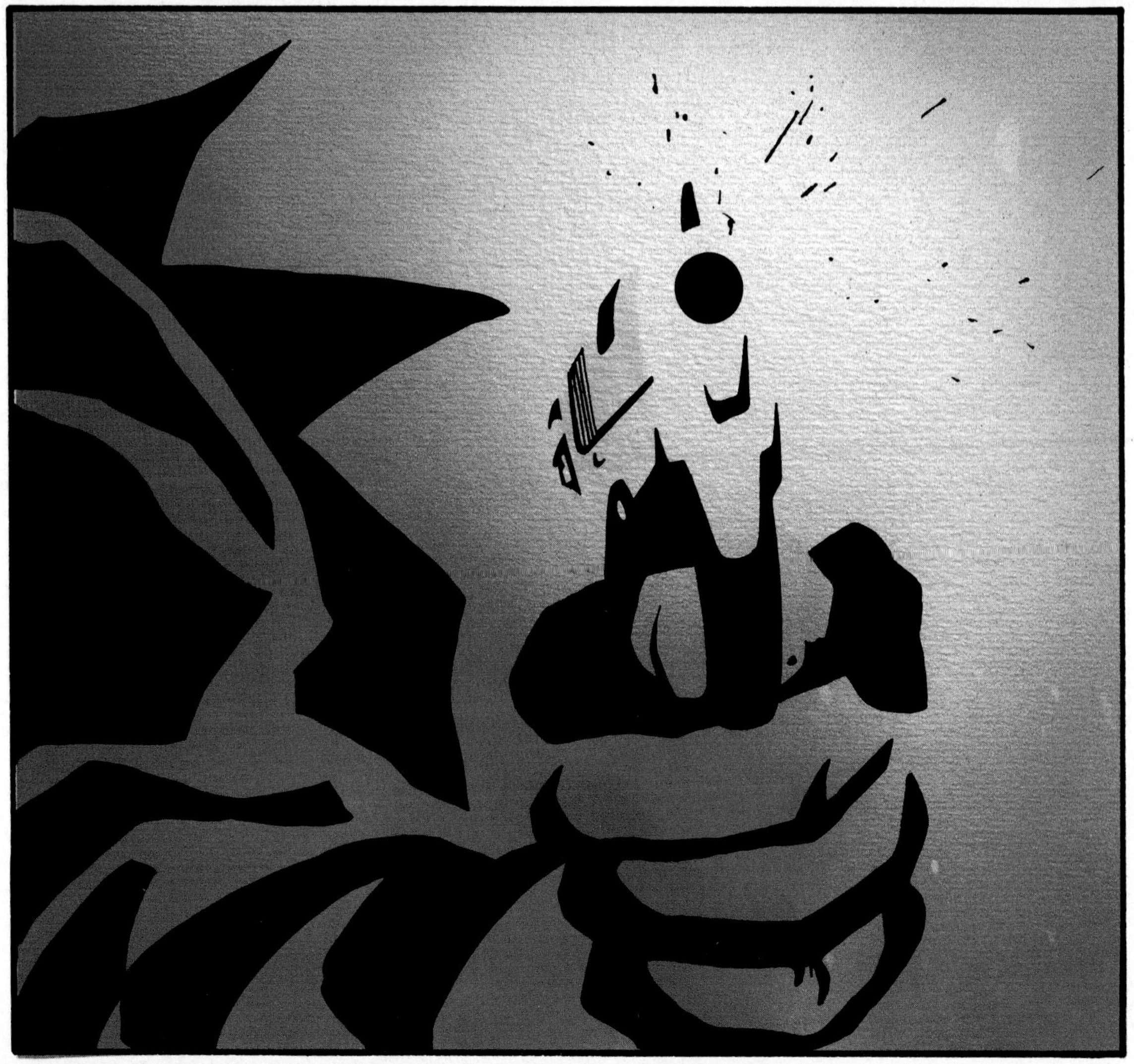

The pebbled-glass door panel is lettered in flaked black paint: "Philip Marlowe... Investigations."
It is a reasonably shabby door at the end of a reasonably shabby corridor in the sort of building that was new about the year the all-tile bathroom became the basis of civilization.

615
PHILIP MARLOWE
INVESTIGATIONS
The door is locked, but next to it is another door with the same legend, which is not locked.

Come on in— there's nobody in here but me.

But not if you're from Manhattan, Kansas.
THAT'S NO WAY TO TALK TO PEOPLE OVER THE PHONE, MISTER MARLOWE.
She had called five minutes before from the drugstore next to my building, but wouldn't tell me what it was she wanted done. I hung up on her when she suggested I try to talk more like a gentleman.

It was a step in the right direction, but it didn't go far enough.
I ought to have locked the door and hidden under the desk.
YOU OUGHT TO BE ASHAMED OF YOURSELF.
I'M JUST TOO PROUD TO SHOW IT. COME ON IN.
IF I TALKED LIKE THAT TO ONE OF DOCTOR ZUGSMITH'S PATIENTS, I'D LOSE MY POSITION.
HOW IS THE OLD BOY?
WHY, SURELY YOU CAN'T KNOW DOCTOR ZUGSMITH.
I KNOW A DOCTOR GEORGE ZUGSMITH. IN SANTA ROSA.
OH, NO. THIS IS DOCTOR ALFRED ZUGSMITH IN MANHATTAN. MANHATTAN, KANSAS, YOU KNOW.
MUST BE A DIFFERENT DOCTOR ZUGSMITH. AND YOUR NAME?

I'M NOT SURE I'D CARE TO TELL YOU. YOU WEREN'T VERY *POLITE* ON THE PHONE.

YOU COULD HAVE SAVED YOURSELF A NICKEL. THE ELEVATOR'S FREE.
I COULDN'T HAVE JUST COME UP HERE--
--WITHOUT KNOWING ANYTHING ABOUT YOU.

JUST WINDOW-SHOPPING, HUH?

THIS IS A VERY... *DELICATE* MATTER. IF I HAVE TO TELL MY FAMILY AFFAIRS TO A TOTAL STRANGER, I AT LEAST HAVE THE RIGHT TO DECIDE WHETHER HE'S THE KIND OF PERSON I COULD TRUST.

IF IT'S THAT DELICATE, MAYBE YOU NEED A LADY DETECTIVE.
GOODNESS, I DIDN'T KNOW THERE WERE ANY.
BUT THAT WOULDN'T DO AT ALL. YOU SEE, ORRIN'S BOARDINGHOUSE WAS IN A VERY TOUGH NEIGHBORHOOD. AT LEAST I THOUGHT IT WAS TOUGH. THE MANAGER SMELLED OF LIQUOR.
DO YOU DRINK, MISTER MARLOWE?

WELL, NOW THAT YOU MENTION IT...
I DON'T THINK I'D CARE TO EMPLOY A DETECTIVE WHO USES LIQUOR. I DON'T EVEN APPROVE OF TOBACCO.

WOULD IT BE ALL RIGHT IF I PEELED AN ORANGE?

WELL, REALLY!

IF YOU HIRE ME, I'M THE GUY YOU HIRE, ME. JUST AS I AM.
I HUNG UP ON YOU, BUT YOU CAME UP HERE ALL THE SAME. SO YOU NEED HELP. WHAT'S YOUR NAME AND TROUBLE?

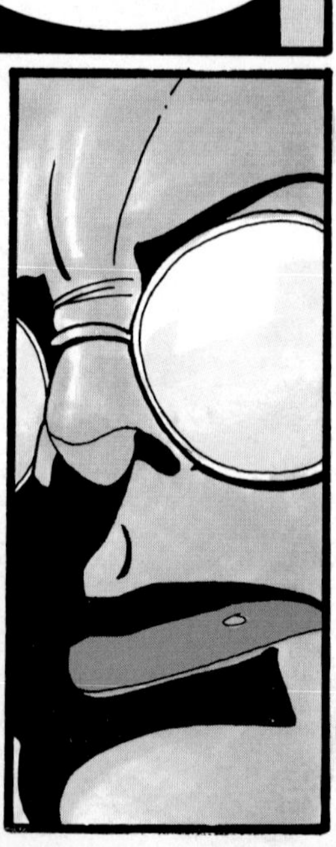

"LOOK, I KNOW YOU WORK FOR DOCTOR ALFRED ZUGSMITH AND YOU'RE LOOKING FOR SOMEBODY NAMED ORRIN. MANHATTAN IS A SMALL TOWN. IT HAS TO BE. ONLY A HALF DOZEN PLACES IN KANSAS ARE ANYTHING ELSE. I ALREADY HAVE ENOUGH INFORMATION ABOUT YOU TO FIND OUT YOUR WHOLE FAMILY HISTORY."
"BUT WHY SHOULD YOU WANT TO?"
"BECAUSE I'M FED UP WITH PEOPLE TELLING ME HISTORIES. I'M JUST SITTING HERE BECAUSE I DON'T HAVE ANYPLACE TO GO."
"YOU TALK TOO MUCH."
CAHUENGA BUILDING
LIQUOR
Yeah, I talk too much. Lonely men always do. Either that or they don't talk at all.
SHALL WE GET DOWN TO BUSINESS?
YOU DON'T LOOK LIKE THE TYPE THAT GOES TO SEE PRIVATE DETECTIVES.
I KNOW THAT. ORRIN WOULD BE LIVID. AND MOTHER, TOO.
I JUST PICKED YOUR NAME OUT OF THE PHONE BOOK AND--
WHAT'S YOUR NAME?!

MY NAME'S ORFAMAY QUEST. MY FATHER WAS A SURGEON. HE DIED FOUR YEARS AGO. I LIVE WITH MY MOTHER, SINCE MY SISTER LEILA AND BROTHER ORRIN LEFT.
ORRIN WAS GOING TO BE A SURGEON, TOO, BUT HE CHANGED TO ENGINEERING AFTER TWO YEARS OF MEDICAL. THEN A YEAR AGO HE CAME OUT TO WORK FOR CAL-WESTERN IN BAY CITY.
HE DIDN'T HAVE TO. I GUESS HE JUST SORT OF WANTED TO COME OUT HERE TO CALIFORNIA. MOST EVERYBODY DOES.
ALMOST EVERYBODY.
IF YOU'RE GOING TO WEAR THOSE RIMLESS GLASSES, AT LEAST TRY TO LIVE UP TO THEM.

"IT WASN'T LIKE ORRIN NOT TO WRITE REGULARLY. BUT THE LAST LETTER WAS SEVERAL MONTHS AGO. MOTHER AND I GOT WORRIED.
"SO IT WAS MY VACATION AND I TOOK THE TRAIN OUT TO SEE HIM. HE'D NEVER BEEN AWAY FROM KANSAS BEFORE.
"AREN'T YOU GOING TO TAKE ANY NOTES?"
"I'LL MAKE THE GAGS, YOU TELL THE STORY. YOU CAME OUT ON YOUR VACATION. THEN WHAT?"
"I'D WRITTEN TO ORRIN THAT I WAS COMING BUT I DIDN'T GET ANY ANSWER. SO ALL I COULD DO WAS GO DOWN TO WHERE HE LIVED. IT'S IN BAY CITY. NUMBER 449 IDAHO STREET.
"IT WAS JUST A CHEAP ROOMING HOUSE. THE MANAGER WAS A HORRID KIND OF MAN. HE SAID ORRIN HAD MOVED AWAY A COUPLE OF WEEKS AGO AND HE DIDN'T KNOW WHERE TO AND HE DIDN'T CARE."
"ALL RIGHT. GO ON."
"WELL, I CALLED THE PLACE WHERE HE WORKED. THE CAL-WESTERN COMPANY, YOU KNOW. AND THEY SAID HE'D BEEN LAID OFF LIKE A LOT OF OTHERS AND THAT WAS ALL THEY KNEW.
"SO THEN I WENT TO THE POST OFFICE AND ASKED IF ORRIN HAD PUT IN A CHANGE OF ADDRESS. THEY SAID NO. SO I BEGAN TO GET A LITTLE FRIGHTENED. HE MIGHT HAVE HAD AN ACCIDENT OR SOMETHING."

DID IT OCCUR TO YOU TO ASK THE POLICE ABOUT THAT?
I WOULDN'T DARE ASK THE POLICE. ORRIN WOULD NEVER FORGIVE ME.
HE'S DIFFICULT ENOUGH IN THE BEST OF TIMES.
She hesitated, and there was something behind her eyes she tried not to have there.
BESIDES, OUR FAMILY'S NOT THE TYPE OF FAMILY TO--
YOU WANT ME TO FINISH YOUR STORY FOR YOU?
HE MOVED. AND YOU DON'T KNOW WHERE HE MOVED TO. AND YOU'RE AFRAID HE'S LIVING A LIFE OF SIN IN SOME PENTHOUSE WITH SOMETHING IN A MINK COAT AND AN INTERESTING PERFUME.
WELL FOR GOODNESS' SAKES!
OR AM I BEING COARSE?

PLEASE, MISTER MARLOW, I DON'T THINK ANYTHING OF THE SORT ABOUT ORRIN. AND IF HE HEARD YOU SAY THAT, YOU'D BE SORRY. HE CAN BE AWFULLY MEAN.
WELL, THEN, JUST WHAT DO YOU THINK MIGHT HAVE HAPPENED?
I GUESS IF I KNEW THAT I WOULDN'T HAVE COME TO SEE YOU.
HOW MUCH WOULD YOU CHARGE TO FIND HIM?

YOU MEAN ALONE, WITHOUT TELLING ANYBODY?

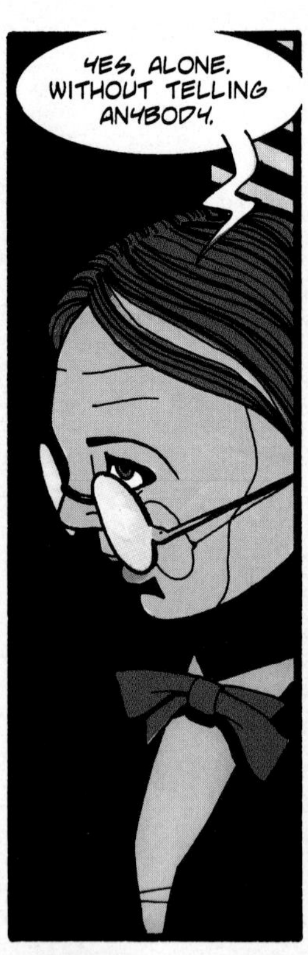
YES, ALONE. WITHOUT TELLING ANYBODY.

UH-HUH.
FORTY BUCKS A DAY AND EXPENSES.

THAT'S FAR TOO MUCH. I COULDN'T POSSIBLY AFFORD MORE THAN TWENTY DOLLARS.
I'VE GOT TO BUY MY MEALS AND MY HOTEL AND THE TRAIN BACK AND--

WHAT HOTEL ARE YOU STAYING AT?

I...I'D RATHER NOT TELL YOU, IF YOU DON'T MIND.
WHY?

I'D JUST RATHER NOT. I'M TERRIBLY AFRAID OF ORRIN'S TEMPER, AND, WELL, I CAN ALWAYS CALL YOU, CAN'T I?

There was a lot I didn't know about her, but there was something in her eyes that was much older than Manhattan, Kansas.
That, and I was just plain bored with doing nothing.

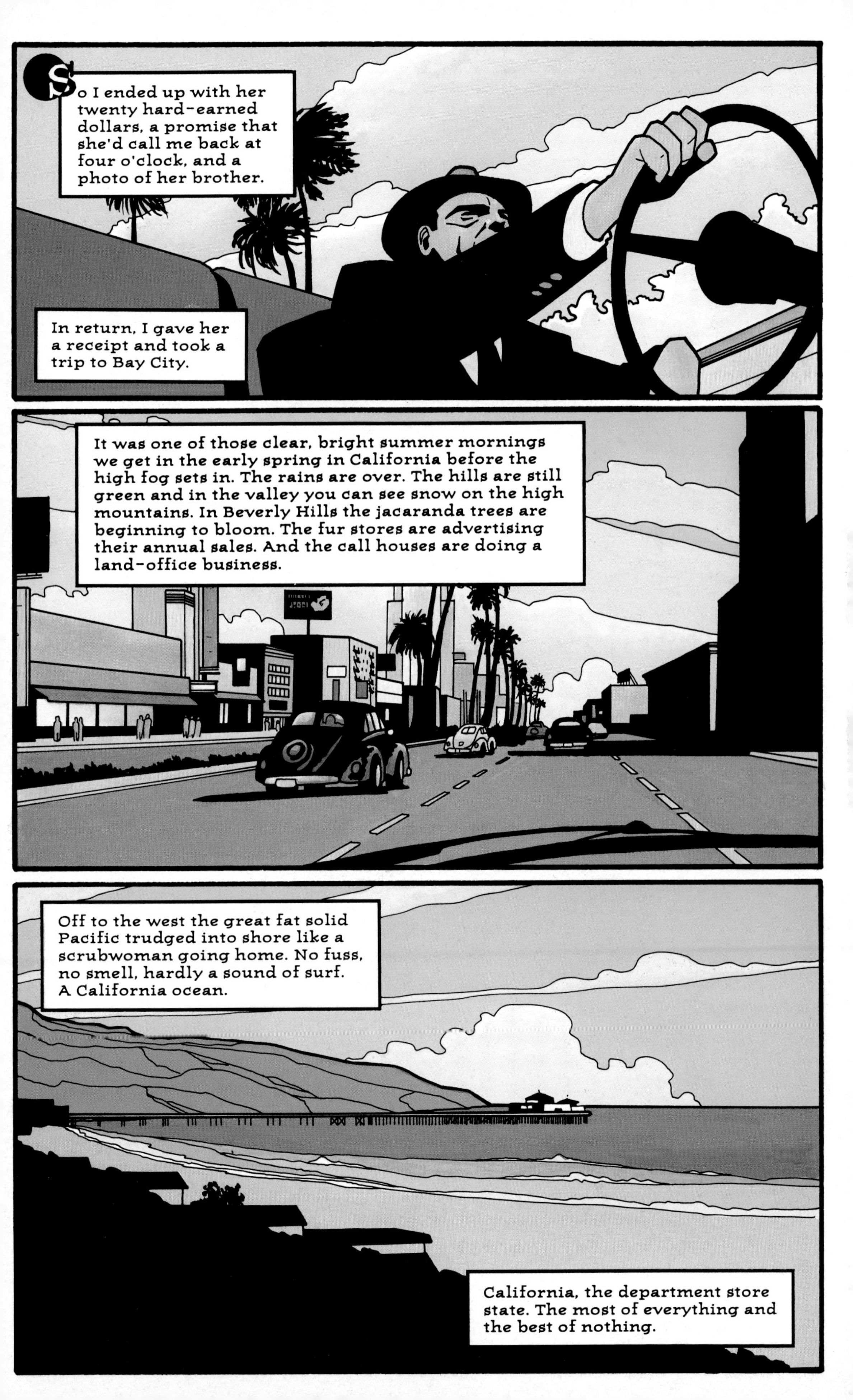
So I ended up with her twenty hard-earned dollars, a promise that she'd call me back at four o'clock, and a photo of her brother.
In return, I gave her a receipt and took a trip to Bay City.
It was one of those clear, bright summer mornings we get in the early spring in California before the high fog sets in. The rains are over. The hills are still green and in the valley you can see snow on the high mountains. In Beverly Hills the jacaranda trees are beginning to bloom. The fur stores are advertising their annual sales. And the call houses are doing a land-office business.
Off to the west the great fat solid Pacific trudged into shore like a scrubwoman going home. No fuss, no smell, hardly a sound of surf. A California ocean.
California, the department store state. The most of everything and the best of nothing.

You could know Bay City a long time without knowing Idaho Street. And you could know a lot of Idaho Street without knowing Number 449.
The "No Vacancies" sign beside the front door had been there a long time. Nothing happened when I rang the bell.
The same nothing happened when I went inside and knocked on the door marked "Manager."
So I prowled around the house and found a door that looked as if it were in the right place for the manager's apartment.
No one seemed to mind my kicking it, either.
The room was full mostly of bad air and gin, but there was a reminiscence of marijuana smoke.
Quest, Orrin P.
The guy on the couch was breathing like an old Ford with a leaky head gasket. Nothing else moved in the neighborhood. Not even a dog.

For some reason I had that empty feeling of having miscounted the trumps.

MMMPH?
NNNG? MMPH! NNNF?

GAAH...! WHO THE HELL'RE YOU?
YOU THE MANAGER?

He nodded and nearly fell off the couch. I poured him a slug of his medicine and he drank it with the beautiful anxiety of a mother welcoming a lost child.
REGISTER
449 IDAHO ST.
GIN
MUS' BE I'M KINDA LITTLE BIT DRUNKY.
YOU'RE NOT BAD. YOU'RE STILL BREATHING.

WHA' GIVES?

I'M LOOKING FOR A MAN NAMED ORRIN P. QUEST.

HUH? MOVED 'WAY.
WHEN?
GIMME A DRINK. I'M NOT HAPPY.

THIS MIGHT HELP YOU CONCENTRATE.

BEAT IT.

I GOT FRIENDS. COUPLE BOYS TAKE CARE A' YOU.
GIN

LEMME TALK A' THE DOC... VINCE! THE DOC!
ISS LESSER B. CLAUSEN, THA'S WHO IT IS! SO YOU JUS' TELL HIM TO...

...TELL HIM TO...
..NNNNGG...
...PWHAAHH...

That was about all he could manage for the time being.

The house was quite silent as I started up the stairs with Lester B. Clausen's passkey.
I paused to write "Vince—Doc" and the phone number I had watched him dial, then let myself into Room 214 without much noise.

It wasn't empty.

I BEG YOUR PARDON. THE MANAGER TOLD ME THIS ROOM WAS VACANT.

YOU CAN ALWAYS TRY KNOCKING.

WHY WOULD I, IF THE MANAGER SAID THE ROOM WAS EMPTY? HE MUST HAVE THOUGHT YOU ALREADY MOVED OUT.
O.K. IF I LOOK AROUND?
THERE'S A "NO VACANCY" SIGN ON THE HOUSE. SO WHAT MAKES YOU THINK YOU COME HERE AND FIND ONE?
MAN NAMED ORRIN P. QUEST TOLD ME ABOUT IT.
I spelled the name for him, but I might as well have been talking to a turtle.

There was a look on his face that you might call watchful. But it was a watchful face to begin with.

YOU AIN'T GETTING NOWHERE WITH THAT BREEZY MANNER, BUB. WHAT KIND OF DICK ARE YOU? CITY?

YOUR GRAMMER'S ALMOST AS LOOSE AS YOUR TOUPÉE.

LAY OFF MY TOUPÉE. WHAT'S THE BEEF?

NO BEEF. I JUST WONDERED WHY YOU HAD THE ROOM.

I MOVED FROM ROOM 215. THIS HERE'S A BETTER ROOM. THAT'S ALL. SATISFIED?

SO YOU'RE HICKS.

"HOW DID YOU--"
"GEORGE W. HICKS. IT'S IN THE REGISTER. ROOM 215. YOU SAID YOU MOVED FROM 215.
"IF YOU HAD A BLACKBOARD I'D WRITE IT OUT FOR YOU."
"DON'T GET TOUGH WITH ME."
"WHAT HAPPENS TO PEOPLE THAT GET TOUGH WITH YOU? YOU MAKE THEM HOLD YOUR TOUPÉE?"
"YOU LAY OFF MY TOUPÉE, IF YOU KNOW WHAT'S GOOD FOR YOU. WHAT'S YOUR CONNECTION?"

I gave him my card and told him I was looking for Orrin P. Quest. He asked why, but I didn't answer.
PHILIP MARLOWE
INVESTIGATIONS
SUITE 615
CAHUENGA BUI
O.K. I'M A CAREFUL GUY MYSELF. THAT'S WHY I'M MOVING OUT.

MAYBE YOU DON'T LIKE REEFER SMOKE.
THAT. AND OTHER THINGS. THAT'S WHY QUEST LEFT. HE WAS A RESPECTABLE TYPE. LIKE ME. I THINK A COUPLE OF HARD BOYS THREW A SCARE INTO HIM.

WHY?
YOU JUST MENTIONED REEFER SMOKE. MAYBE HE WENT TO HEAD-QUARTERS.

IN BAY CITY? WHY WOULD HE BOTHER?

WELL, THANKS A LOT, MISTER HICKS. GOING FAR?
JUST FAR ENOUGH.
WHAT'S YOUR RACKET, ANYWAY?
RACKET?
WHAT DO YOU SHAKE THEM FOR? HOW DO YOU MAKE YOUR DIBS?

YOU GOT ME WRONG, BROTHER. I'M A RETIRED OPTOMETRIST.

THAT WHY YOU HAVE THE GUN IN THERE?
WHAT, THAT? IT'S BEEN IN THE FAMILY FOR YEARS.

PRIVATE DETECTIVE, HUH? SO, UH, WHAT KIND OF WORK YOU DO MOSTLY?

ANYTHING THAT'S REASONABLY HONEST.

REASONABLY IS A WORD YOU COULD STRETCH. SO'S HONEST.
YOU'RE SO RIGHT. LET'S GET TOGETHER SOME QUIET AFTERNOON AND STRETCH THEM.

I don't know what I expected to hear after I left, but whatever it was I didn't hear it.
I made a lot of noise going along the hall to the head of the stairs, then went quietly back to Room 215 and used the passkey to enter. Somewhere a door closed, and a car drove away from the front of the house.
No more than two minutes passed before Hicks was on his way. He was so quiet that if I hadn't been listening for him, I wouldn't have heard him go downstairs and slip into the manager's apartment.

I made another pilgrimage to Room 214. I searched with care and patience, but found nothing that connected it in any way with Orrin P. Quest. There was no reason why I should.

MANAGER
Orrin P. Quest had moved away. Somebody had taken over his room. Somebody else had the room registered to Hicks.

The party on the floor went nicely with the neighborhood. The fact that he sold reefers on the side was a social eccentricity that would cause no comment at all on Idaho Street.
I didn't think it would be much of a problem to sift out the party that went by the name "Doc" or "Vince" at the phone number I had watched him dial.
But first I wanted to go back through the register.
It wasn't up to date, but I—
The page with Orrin Quest's registration had been torn out.
A careful man, Mr. George W. Hicks. Very careful.

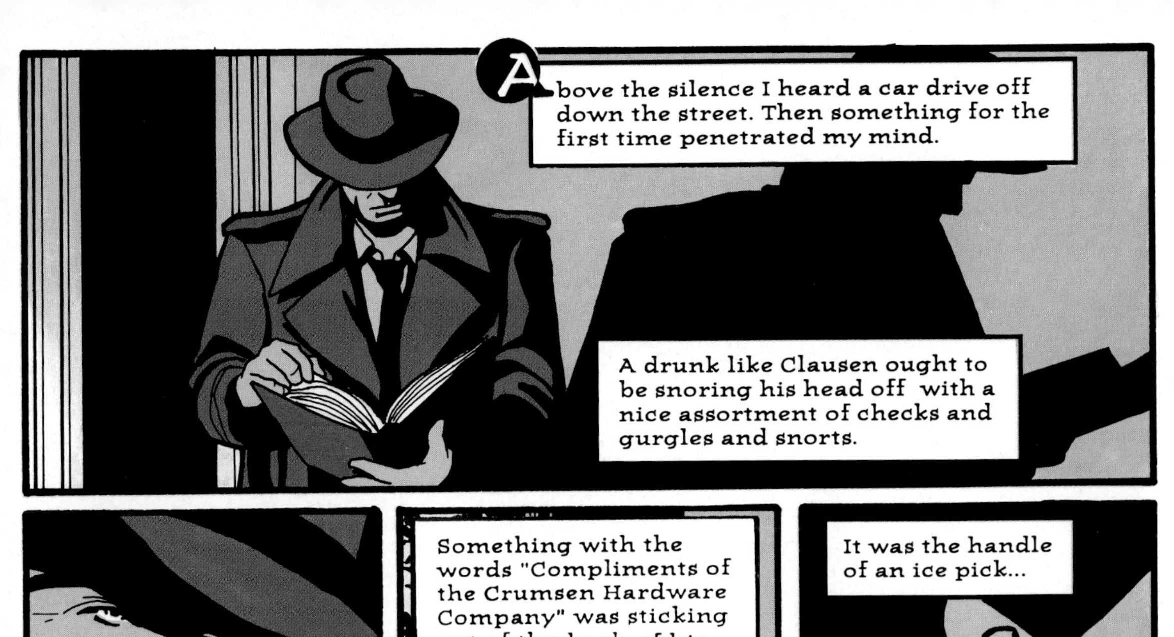
Above the silence I heard a car drive off down the street. Then something for the first time penetrated my mind.
A drunk like Clausen ought to be snoring his head off with a nice assortment of checks and gurgles and snorts.

He wasn't making a sound.

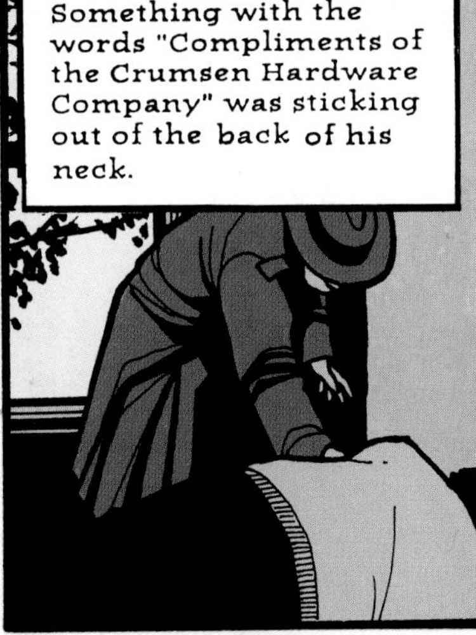
Something with the words "Compliments of the Crumsen Hardware Company" was sticking out of the back of his neck.

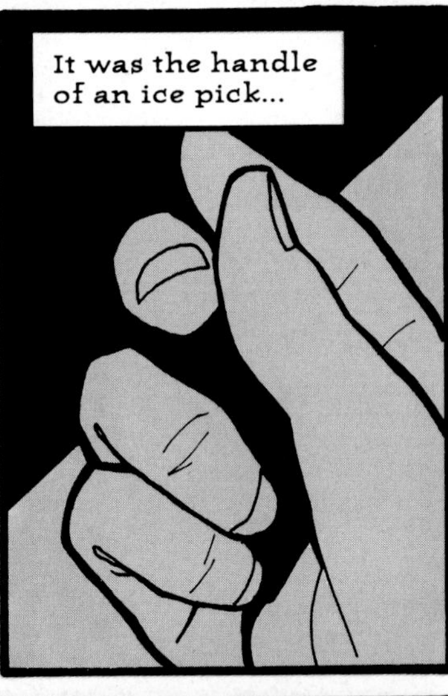
It was the handle of an ice pick...

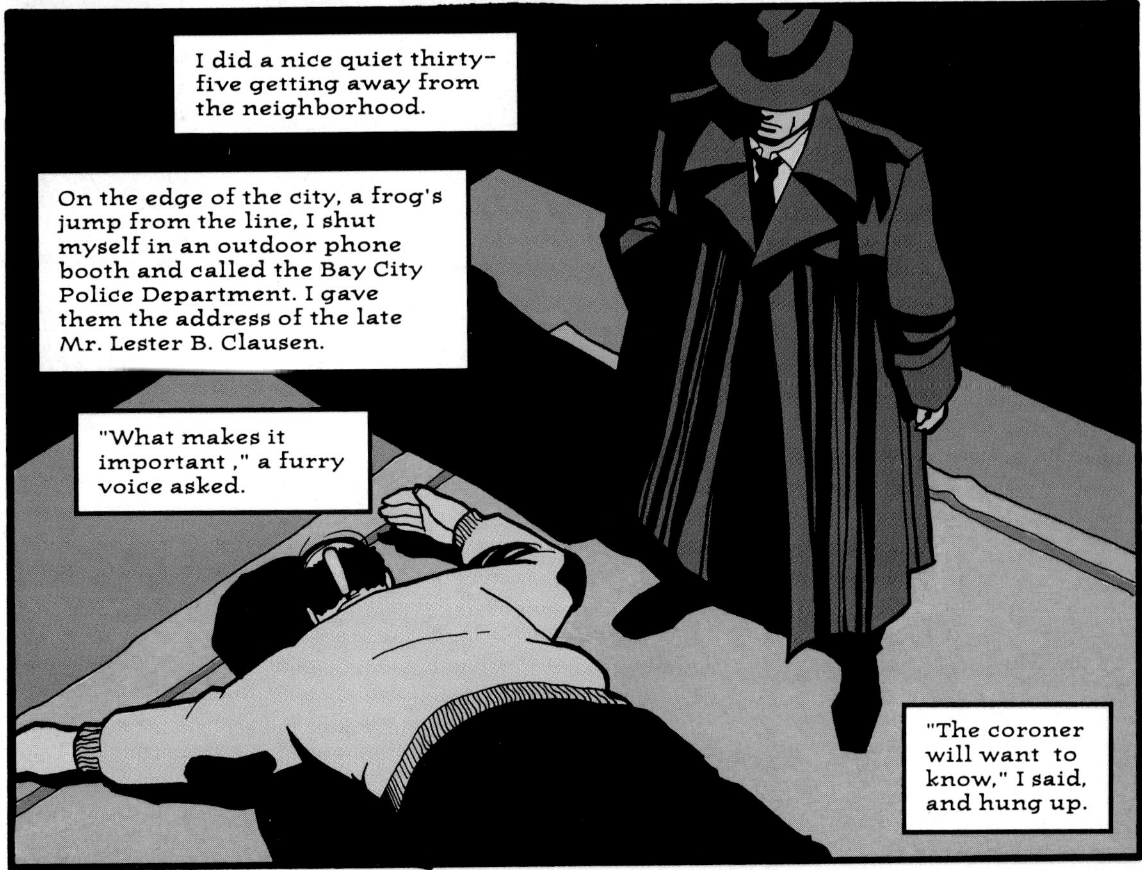
I did a nice quiet thirty-five getting away from the neighborhood.
On the edge of the city, a frog's jump from the line, I shut myself in an outdoor phone booth and called the Bay City Police Department. I gave them the address of the late Mr. Lester B. Clausen.
"What makes it important," a furry voice asked.
"The coroner will want to know," I said, and hung up.

Back in Hollywood it took me a quarter-hour to match up the number Clausen had dialed with a Dr. Vincent Lagardie, who called himself a neurologist.
I went to the drugstore around the corner and gave him a call.
When I finally got through to him his voice was very impatient.
"WELL, DOCTOR LAGARDIE, IF YOU DON'T KNOW MISTER CLAUSEN, THAT'S ALL RIGHT THEN. JUST WANTED TO MAKE SURE. SOMEBODY STUCK AN ICE PICK IN THE BACK OF HIS NECK."
The doctor didn't seem to be in so much of a hurry now.
HAS THIS BEEN REPORTED TO THE POLICE?
NATURALLY. BUT IT SHOULDN'T BOTHER YOU, UNLESS IT WAS YOUR ICE PICK.
AND WHO IS THIS SPEAKING?
3 MIN LIMIT
THE NAME'S HICKS. GEORGE W. HICKS.
I'M SORRY, MISTER HICKS, BUT I DON'T KNOW MISTER CLAUSEN, NOR HAVE I EVER HEARD OF HIM. AND I HAVE AN EXCELLENT MEMORY FOR NAMES.
WELL, THAT'S FINE. BUT SOMEBODY MAY WANT TO KNOW WHY HE TRIED TO TELEPHONE YOU--UNLESS I FORGOT TO PASS THAT INFORMATION ALONG.

COFFEE
SHOPPE
He didn't have any comment to make on that, and neither did I. If he was on the level, he would now telephone the Bay City Police and tell them the story.
If he didn't, he wasn't on the level. Which might or might not be useful to know.

"AREN'T YOU EVER NICE TO ANYBODY?"
"NOTHING I SAY IS NICE. I'M NOT NICE. BY YOUR STANDARDS NOBODY WITH LESS THAN THREE PRAYER BOOKS IS NICE."
The phone on my desk had rung at four o'clock sharp. She was in the drugstore again. I told her to come on up and stop acting like Mata Hari.

ALL I COULD FIND OUT IS THAT THE DUMP ON IDAHO STREET IS PEDDLING REEFERS. THAT'S MARIJUANA CIGARETTES.
WHY, HOW DIGUSTING.

WE HAVE TO TAKE THE GOOD WITH THE BAD IN THIS LIFE. ORRIN MUST HAVE GOT WISE AND THREATENED TO REPORT IT TO THE POLICE. SO THEY THREW A SCARE INTO HIM.

OH, THEY COULDN'T SCARE ORRIN, MISTER MARLOWE. ORRIN JUST GETS MEAN WHEN PEOPLE TRY TO RUN HIM.

OKAY. SO THEY DIDN'T SCARE HIM.
SAY THEY JUST CUT OFF ONE OF HIS LEGS AND BEAT HIM OVER THE HEAD WITH IT.
WHAT WOULD HE DO THEN--WRITE THE BETTER BUSINESS BUREAU?

ARE YOU TRYING TO FRIGHTEN ME, MISTER MARLOWE?
IF I AM I'M GETTING NOWHERE FAST.

MISTER MARLOWE, I PAID YOU TWENTY DOLLARS FOR A DAY'S WORK. ALL YOU'VE DONE IS FIND OUT THAT ORRIN LIVED IN A BAD NEIGHBORHOOD. I FOUND THAT OUT MYSELF. IT DOESN'T SEEM TO ME YOU'VE DONE A DAY'S WORK.

DON'T BOTHER ABOUT THE TWENTY BUCKS. I DIDN'T EVEN BRUISE IT.
BUT THE DAY'S NOT OVER YET, AND I'M DOING ALL I CAN WITH THE FACTS I HAVE.
I DON'T THINK SO.
BUT I'VE TOLD YOU ALL I KNOW.
WELL, I'M SURE I CAN'T HELP WHAT YOU THINK.

HOW OFTEN DID ORRIN WRITE? BEFORE HE STOPPED?
EVERY WEEK. SOMETIMES OFTENER.
ABOUT WHAT?
YOU MEAN WHAT DID HE WRITE ABOUT?

WHAT DO YOU THINK I MEANT?
WELL YOU DON'T HAVE TO SNAP AT ME. HE WROTE ABOUT HIS WORK AND THE PLANT AND SOMETIMES ABOUT A SHOW HE'D BEEN TO. SOMETIMES IT WAS ABOUT CHURCH.
NOTHING ABOUT GIRLS?

I DON'T THINK HE CARED MUCH FOR GIRLS.
WHAT DID HE DO FOR FUN?
HE...HE STUDIES A LOT, AND--
THAT'S IT?

HE HAS THIS EXPENSIVE CAMERA HE LIKES TO SNAP PEOPLE WITH WHEN THEY AREN'T LOOKING.

AND HE STOPPED WRITING HOW LONG AGO?
WELL, ABOUT THREE OR FOUR MONTHS.
WHAT WAS THE DATE OF HIS LAST LETTER?

I...I'M AFRAID I CAN'T TELL YOU EXACTLY. BUT IT WAS LIKE I TOLD YOU--

I KNOW WHAT YOU TOLD ME. NOW I'LL TELL YOU WHAT'S WRONG WITH THIS PICTURE.

"WHAT'S WRONG IS THAT YOU'RE NOT SCARED. NEITHER YOU OR YOUR MOTHER. AND YOU OUGHT TO BE SCARED AS HELL.
"I CAN'T SEE MYSELF WAITING FOR MY SUMMER VACATION TO COME AROUND BEFORE I START ASKING QUESTIONS. I CAN'T SEE MYSELF BY-PASSING THE POLICE."

I CAN'T SEE YOUR DEAR OLD MOTHER SITTING THERE IN MANHATTAN, NO LETTER FROM ORRIN, NO NEWS, AND ALL SHE DOES IS TAKE A LONG BREATH AND MEND UP ANOTHER PAIR OF THE MINISTER'S PANTS.

YOU'RE A HORRID, DISGUSTING MAN. DON'T YOU DARE SAY MOTHER AND I WEREN'T WORRIED.
JUST DON'T YOU DARE.

YOU WERE WORRIED TWENTY DOLLARS' WORTH.

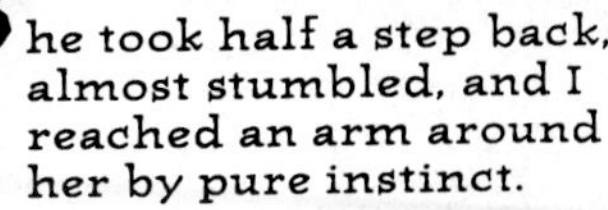
She took half a step back, almost stumbled, and I reached an arm around her by pure instinct.

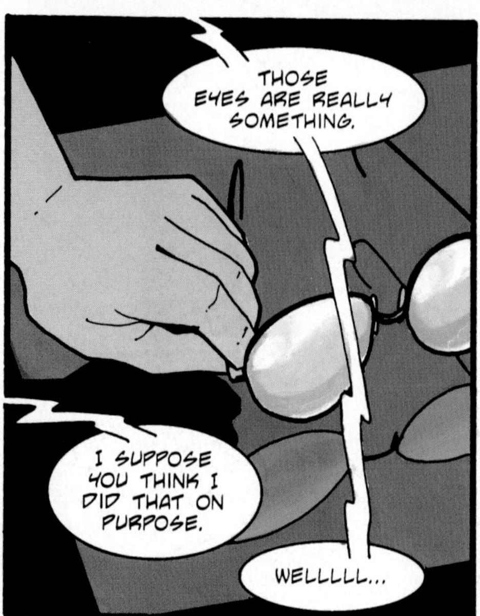
THOSE EYES ARE REALLY SOMETHING.
I SUPPOSE YOU THINK I DID THAT ON PURPOSE.
WELLLLL...

She reached a quick arm around my neck and started to pull, so I kissed her.It was either that or slug her.

DO YOU DO THIS TO ALL THE CUSTOMERS?
I JUST DIDN'T WANT YOU TO LOSE YOUR BALANCE.
I KNEW YOU WERE THE THOUGHTFUL TYPE.

I'M SORRY I WAS MEAN. I THINK YOU'RE VERY NICE, REALLY. I'LL CALL YOU.

Out she went, tap tap tap, down the hall.
The phone rang before I had quite started to worry about the late Mr. Lester B. Clausen. The voice on the other end was thick and clogged, as if it were being strangled by a curtain.

YOU MARLOWE?
SPEAKING.
YOU GOT A SAFE-DEPOSIT BOX, MARLOWE?

I had enough being polite for one afternoon.
IF YOU GOT A PROPOSITION, STATE IT.
AND I GET CALLED "MISTER" UNTIL YOU GIVE ME SOME MONEY.

DON'T LET THAT TEMPER RIDE YOU SO HARD, FRIEND. I NEED SOMETHING KEPT IN A SAFE PLACE. FOR THAT I GOT A C-NOTE RIGHT HERE AND WAITING.

RIGHT HERE AND WAITING?
ROOM 332, VAN NUYS HOTEL. KNOCK TWO QUICK ONES AND TWO SLOW ONES.

WHAT'S YOUR NAME?
JUST ROOM 332.
THANKS FOR THE TIME. GOOD-BYE.

HEY, WAIT A MINUTE.

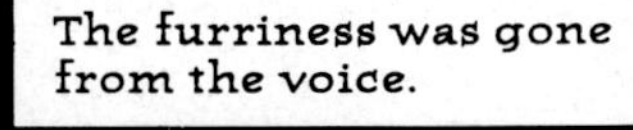
The furriness was gone from the voice.
HOW'S EVERY LITTLE THING IN BAY CITY, MARLOWE?
It took me twenty-nine minutes to get to the Van Nuys Hotel.

Once, long ago, it must have had a certain elegance. But no more.
The memories of old cigars hung to its ceiling and the sagging springs of its leather lounge chairs.
Room 332 was at the back of the corridor, near the door to the fire escape. The hall that led to it had a smell of old furniture oil and the drab anonymity of a thousand shabby lives.
The hotel dick, a real dope by the name of Flack, told me that the party in Room 332 had checked in at 2:47 P.M. under the name of Dr. G. W. Hambleton, El Centro, California.
DOCTOR HAMBLETON?
332
Of course I had to pry it out of him. There are days like that. Everybody you meet is a dope. You begin to look at yourself in the mirror and wonder.

DOCTOR HAMBLETON?
I felt jaded and old. I felt as if I had spent my life knocking at doors in cheap hotels that nobody bothered to open.

TURN AROUND AND PUT YOUR HANDS BEHIND YOU.

It was not the voice that had talked to me on the telephone. But it was a voice I'd heard before.

DON'T THINK
I'M FOOLING. I'LL
GIVE YOU THREE
SECONDS.

COULDN'T
YOU MAKE IT
A MINUTE? I LIKE
LOOKING AT
YOU.

ALL RIGHT.
IF THAT'S THE WAY
YOU WANT IT.

Something had hit me
on the back of the head,
but it didn't feel like a
gun butt.

I climbed to my feet and went into the bathroom to wash off the blood.
I wondered why I didn't run after her screaming.

But what I was doing was staring into the open medicine cabinet over the basin.
Someone had been looking for something.

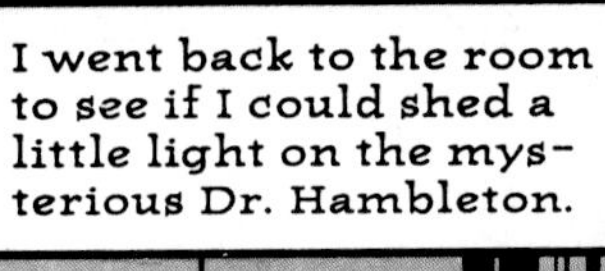
I went back to the room to see if I could shed a little light on the mysterious Dr. Hambleton.

He had been there all along, but hadn't moved, for a somewhat obvious reason.

Someone had stuck an ice-pick in the back of his neck.
He was wearing a toupée. Last time I had talked to him his name had been George W. Hicks. Same initials. Not that it mattered anymore. I wasn't going to be talking to him again.

I wondered what his mistake had been. He had seemed a fairly wise bird.

The point of interest now was whether the people who had ice-picked Dr. Hambleton had found what they came for.
The desk had been searched. The Gideon Bible was thrown in a corner. The telephone bell box had been left open. The ribbon bow of his hat had been picked with a knife point.

So this was the take. If the killers knew what they were looking for, it was something that could be hidden in a book, a telephone box, a tube of toothpaste, or a hatband.

Or...

...under a toupée.

They had had very little time. It hadn't been much more than a half hour since I had gotten the phone call.

I didn't see a way out of getting the cops involved in this one, so I went to talk to my pal Flack. I had the feeling he hadn't seen a first-class ice pick job lately.
BAY CITY CAMERA SHOP
Nº 762
George W. Hicks
449 Idaho Street
Bay City
enlarged Prints from Negative

"PUNCTURED SPINAL CORD JUST BELOW THE OCCIPITAL BULGE, I'D SAY. VERY VULNERABLE SPOT, IF YOU KNOW HOW TO FIND IT. WHOEVER DID THIS ONE WAS A PERFORMER. GOT THE SPINAL CORD ON THE FIRST TRY."
VAN NUYS

AND ANOTHER THING--YOU HAVE TO HAVE THE GUY *QUIET* TO DO IT. THAT MEANS MORE THAN ONE KILLER, UNLESS HE WAS DOPED, OR THE KILLER WAS A FRIEND OF HIS.
I DON'T SEE HOW HE COULD HAVE BEEN DOPED, IF HE'S THE PARTY THAT CALLED ME ON THE PHONE.
mpliments of
SEN HARDWARE Co
L.A.P.D.

IF, AND SINCE YOU DIDN'T KNOW THE GUY-- ACCORDING TO YOU--THERE'S ALWAYS THE FAINT POSSIBILITY THAT YOU WOULDN'T KNOW HIS VOICE. OR AM I BEING TOO SUBTLE?
I DON'T KNOW. I HAVEN'T READ YOUR FAN MAIL.
DON'T WASTE IT ON HIM, FRENCH.

DON'T YOU EVER READ A PAPER, FLACK? MOYER'S A GENTLEMAN NOW. EVEN HAS ANOTHER NAME. GENTLEMEN HIRE THINGS DONE.

AND AS FOR THE STEIN JOB, WE HAD HIM IN JAIL AT THE TIME ON A GAMBLING RAP. WE DIDN'T GET ANYWHERE, BUT WE GAVE HIM A VERY SWEET ALIBI.

ALL RIGHT. THE CUSTOMER HAD SOMETHING HE WAS AFRAID TO KEEP AROUND. THAT MEANS HE KNEW SOMEBODY WAS AFTER HIM AND GETTING CLOSE. SO HE OFFERS MARLOWE A HUNDRED BUCKS TO KEEP IT FOR HIM.
IT MUST HAVE BEEN SOMETHING SEMI-LEGITIMATE. THAT RIGHT, MARLOWE?
YOU COULD LEAVE OUT THE SEMI.

SO WHAT HE HAD WAS SOMETHING THAT COULD BE KEPT FLAT OR ROLLED UP, AND WE DON'T KNOW WHETHER IT WAS FOUND OR NOT.
ANY CHANCE TO CHECK HIS VISITORS?
YOU DON'T EVEN HAVE TO PASS THE DESK TO GET THE ELEVATORS.
MAYBE THAT'S WHY HE CAME HERE. THAT, AND THE HOMEY ATMOSPHERE.

NOW, WAIT A MINUTE--!
YOU MUSTN'T DENY US OUR LITTLE PLEASURES, MISTER FLACK.
OKAY. WHOEVER KNOCKED HIM OFF COULD COME AND GO WITHOUT ANY QUESTION ASKED. AND THAT'S ABOUT ALL WE KNOW. OKAY, BEIFUS?
NOT QUITE ALL.

Without the toupée, Beifus and French realized that Dr. Hambleton was really Mileaway Marston, who used to be a runner for a gangster by the name of Ace Devore.
They knew that a dead two-bit punk wasn't going to be a twenty-four-hour-a-day job. That took a load off their minds. But not mine.
So I placed a call to a man I knew named Peoria Smith, a studio grifter in the business of selling unlisted addresses and phone numbers.

Movie stars' unlisted addresses and phone numbers.
ARE YOU QUITE SURE YOU HAVE THE STILLS, *AMIGO?* THEY ARE USUALLY A LITTLE TOO BIG TO PUT IN YOUR POCKET.
FOR MISS WELD PERSONALLY. SORRY.
I TOLD YOU SHE WAS TAKING A BATH.
I'LL WAIT.
LIFE
MAVIS WELD:
To Mavis: Best Wishes. Humphrey
I SEE. I AM MOST FULLY AWARE THAT YOU ARE A GODDAM LIAR AND THAT YOU HAVE NO STILLS IN YOUR POCKETS. NOT THAT I WISH TO INQUIRE INTO YOUR NO DOUBT VERY PRIVATE BUSINESS.
YEAH?
PERHAPS YOU WOULD LIKE TO HELP HER. THE BATHROOM IS OVER THERE, THROUGH THE ARCH AND TO THE RIGHT. MOST PROBABLY THE DOOR IS NOT LOCKED.
NOT IF IT'S THAT EASY.

OH, YOU LIKE TO DO THE DIFFICULT THINGS IN LIFE. I MUST REMEMBER TO BE LESS APPROACHABLE.

DON'T BOTHER, MISS GONZALES. I'M JUST A GUY WHO CAME HERE ON BUSINESS.

YOU ARE AN AMUSING SON OF A BITCH. YOU MAY CALL ME DOLORES, IF YOU WISH.

I felt her hand in my breast pocket.

Before I could stop her, she snatched my wallet with fingers that darted like little snakes.

SO GLAD YOU TWO GOT ACQUAINTED.

It was the voice I'd heard at the hotel, only this time there was no towel or dark cheaters. But it was the same girl, all right, glasses on or off.

THE NAME IS PHILLIP MARLOWE. NICE, DON'T YOU THINK?

I DIDN'T KNOW YOU BOTHERED TO ASK THEM THEIR NAMES. YOU SELDOM KNOW THEM LONG ENOUGH.

SUCH A CHARMING WAY TO CALL A GIRL A WHORE.
AT LEAST I HAVEN'T BEEN SLEEPING WITH ANY GUNMEN LATELY.

ARE YOU SURE?
OPEN THE DOOR, HONEY. THIS IS THE DAY WE PUT THE GARBAGE OUT.

The Gonzales looked back at her slowly, levelly and with a knife in her eyes.

Then she yanked the door wide and closed it with a jarring smash.

The noise didn't even flicker the steady dark blue glare in Mavis Weld's eyes.
NOW, SUPPOSE YOU DO THE SAME--BUT MORE QUIETLY.

I CAME HERE ON BUSINESS, MISS WELD.

YES. I CAN IMAGINE. MAKE WITH THE FEET, DREAMBOAT. I DON'T KNOW YOU. I DON'T WANT TO KNOW YOU. AND IF I DID, THIS WOULDN'T BE EITHER THE DAY OR THE HOUR.
"NEVER THE TIME AND THE PLACE AND THE LOVED ONE ALL TOGETHER."

"WHAT'S THAT?"
"BROWNING. THE POET, NOT THE AUTOMATIC. I FEEL SURE YOU'D PREFER THE AUTOMATIC."

DO I HAVE TO CALL THE MANAGER TO BOUNCE YOU OUT OF HERE LIKE A BASKETBALL?

IF YOU'RE GOING TO STAND THAT CLOSE TO ME, MAYBE YOU'D BETTER PUT SOME CLOTHES ON.

DID I HURT YOU?
THAT'S FINE.
YEAH.

I THINK YOU'D BETTER KISS ME.

BELIEVE ME. THERE'S ONLY ONE REASON I DON'T.
EVEN IF YOU HAD YOUR LITTLE BLACK GUN WITH YOU.

OR THE BRASS KNUCKLES YOU PROBABLY KEEP ON YOUR NIGHT TABLE.

IF I CAN'T SCARE YOU, OR LICK YOU, OR SEDUCE YOU, WHAT THE HELL CAN I BUY YOU WITH?
OH, A HUNDRED BUCKS TO START WITH.
YOU'RE CHEAP. IS A HUNDRED BUCKS MONEY IN YOUR CIRCLE, DARLING?
MAKE IT TWO HUNDRED, THEN. I COULD RETIRE ON THAT.

AND WHAT WOULD I GET FOR THIS MONEY, MY CHARMING LITTLE GUM-SHOE?
YOU'D GET A RECEIPT. WHO TOLD YOU I WAS A GUM-SHOE?
IT MUST HAVE BEEN THE SMELL.

I'M BEGINNING TO THINK YOU WRITE YOUR OWN DIALOGUE. I'VE BEEN WONDERING JUST WHAT WAS THE MATTER WITH IT.

AND WITH THAT, I BELIEVE I MUST HAVE USED UP MY ENTIRE STOCK OF GIRLISH CHARM.

I NEVER THOUGHT YOU KILLED HIM. BUT IT WOULD HELP TO HAVE SOME SORT OF REASON FOR NOT TELLING ME YOU WERE THERE.
IT'S A HELP TO HAVE ENOUGH MONEY FOR A RETAINER JUST TO ESTABLISH MYSELF. AND ENOUGH INFORMATION TO JUSTIFY MY ACCEPTING THE RETAINER.

MY GOODNESS. AM I SUPPOSED TO HAVE KILLED SOMEBODY?

LOOK, YOU'RE GOING TO FIND THIS HARD TO BELIEVE. BUT I CAME OVER HERE WITH THE QUAINT IDEA THAT YOU MIGHT BE A GIRL WHO NEEDED SOME HELP.

I FIGURED YOU WENT TO THAT HOTEL ROOM TO MAKE SOME KIND OF A PAYOFF.
AND THE FACT THAT YOU WENT BY YOURSELF AND TOOK CHANCES ON BEING RECOGNIZED MADE ME THINK YOU MIGHT BE IN ONE OF THOSE HOLLYWOOD JAMS THAT REALLY MEAN CURTAINS.

LIFE
BUT YOU'RE NOT IN ANY JAM. YOU'RE RIGHT UP FRONT UNDER THE BABY SPOT PULLING EVERY TIRED HAM GESTURE YOU EVER USED IN THE MOST TIRED "B" PICTURE YOU EVER ACTED IN--IF ACTING IS THE WORD.
MAVIS WELD:

SHUT UP. SHUT UP, YOU SLIMY, BLACKMAILING KEYHOLE PEEPER.

YOU DON'T NEED ME. YOU DON'T NEED ANYBODY. YOU'RE SO GODDAMNED SMART YOU COULD TALK YOUR WAY OUT OF A SAFE-DEPOSIT BOX.
OKAY. GO AHEAD AND TALK YOUR WAY OUT. I WON'T STOP YOU. JUST DON'T MAKE ME LISTEN TO IT.

She didn't move or breathe when I reached the door, nor when I opened it. I don't know why. The stuff wasn't *that* good.
CRESTVIEW COURTS

I thought about a picture show I'd seen that had Mavis Weld in it. One of those glass-and-chromium deals where everybody smiled too much and knew it.
The women were always going up a long curving staircase to change their clothes. The men were always taking monogrammed cigarettes out of expensive cases and snapping expensive lighters at each other.
Mavis Weld played second lead and she played it with wraps on. She was good, but she could have been ten times better.

But if she had been, half her scenes would have been yanked out to protect the star. It was as neat a bit of tightrope walking as I ever saw.

Well it wouldn't be a tightrope she'd be walking from now on. It would be piano wire. It would be very high.
And there wouldn't be any net under it.
MISTER MARLOWE, NO DOUBT?

MY NAME'S TOAD. JOSEPH P. TOAD.
IT'S A LITTLE LATE FOR A BUSINESS CALL. I HOPE YOU DON'T MIND.

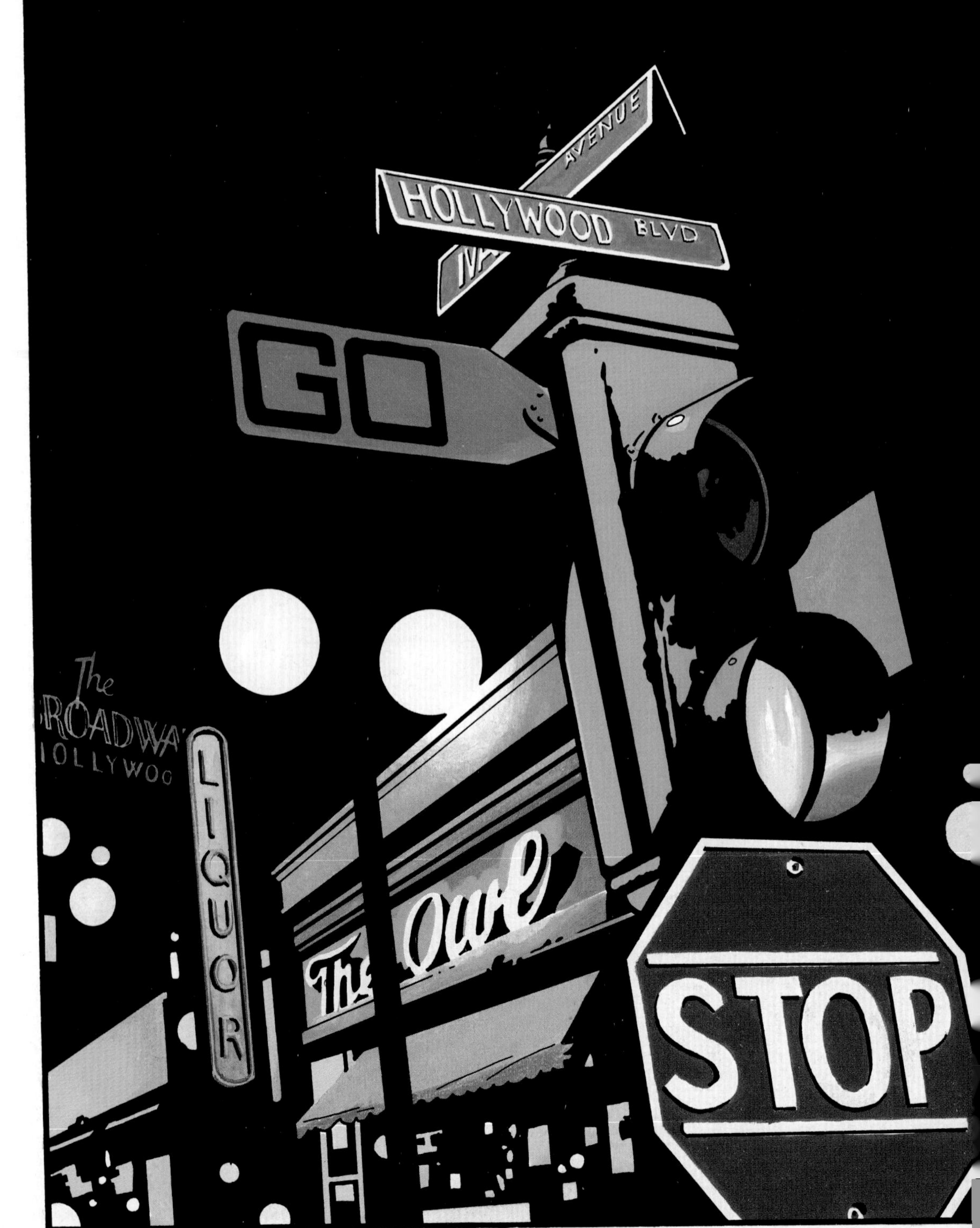
AVENUE
HOLLYWOOD BLVD
GO
The
LIQUOR
The Owl
STOP

Most of the doors were dark in the corridor, but not all.
People work nights in businesses other than mine.
The noise of the building, except the sound of the scrubwomen still cleaning up the debris of the wasted hours, seemed to have flowed out into the street and lost itself among the turning wheels of innumerable cars.

Then somewhere along the hall outside a man started whistling "Lili Marlene" with elegance and virtuosity.

615
PHILIP MARLOWE
INVESTIGATIONS
Although at that moment, I wasn't paying much attention...

I TRUST YOU DON'T ALREADY HAVE ALL THE BUSINESS YOU CAN HANDLE, MISTER MARLOWE?

DON'T KID ME. MY NERVES ARE FRAYED.
WHO'S THE JUNKIE WITH THE GUN?

COME ALONG, ALFRED. AND STOP ACTING GIRLISH.

SCREW YOU.

QUITE A PROBLEM, THIS ALFRED. I GOT HIM OFF THE STUFF, TEMPORARILY AT LEAST.
I wondered just what he was off of. His nose twitched and his mouth twitched and his hands twitched.
But there was nothing nervous about his movements with the gun.

SAY HELLO TO MISTER MARLOWE, ALFRED.
SCREW HIM.

The gun pointed at my chest.

His finger tightened around the trigger. I watched it tighten.

I knew at precisely what moment that tightening would release the hammer.

It didn't seem to make any difference.

This was happening somewhere else—
—in a cheesy program picture.

It wasn't happening to me.

Then the hammer of the automatic clicked dryly on nothing.

I GOT THE MAGAZINE.
ALFRED AIN'T RELIABLE LATELY. THE LITTLE BASTARD MIGHT HAVE SHOT YOU.

I let my heels down on the floor again.
COME ON INTO MY PARLOR.

YOU DON'T HAVE A COMIC BOOK AROUND, DO YOU? KEEPS HIM QUIET.
SIT DOWN. I'LL LOOK.

YOU WON'T NEED THAT.

THAT'S FINE. BUT IF I DO, HERE IT IS.

MAYBE WE PLAYED THIS WRONG.
MIND IF I PUT MY HAND IN MY POCKET? I DON'T WEAR A GUN.

FIVE C'S. FOR NOTHING AT ALL BUT KEEPING THE NOSE CLEAN. CHECK?

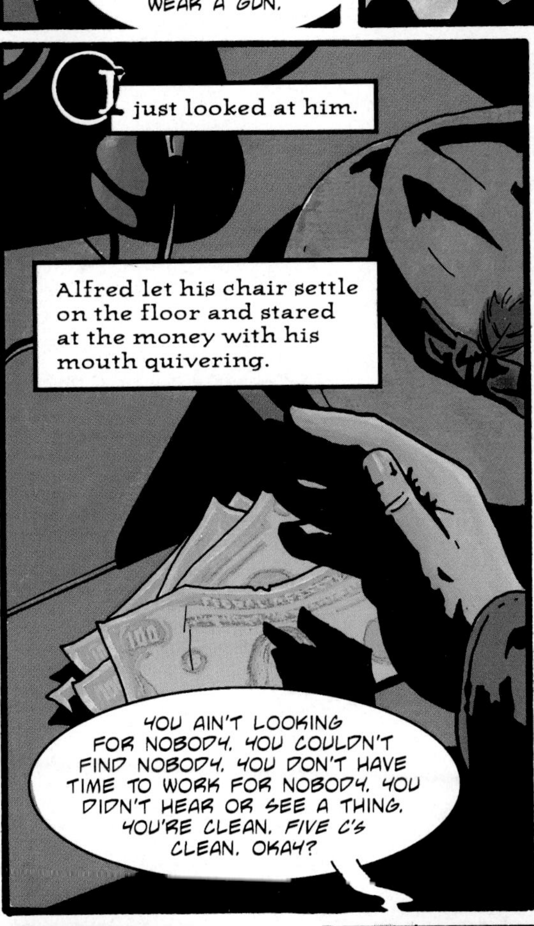
I just looked at him.
Alfred let his chair settle on the floor and stared at the money with his mouth quivering.
YOU AIN'T LOOKING FOR NOBODY. YOU COULDN'T FIND NOBODY. YOU DON'T HAVE TIME TO WORK FOR NOBODY. YOU DIDN'T HEAR OR SEE A THING. YOU'RE CLEAN. FIVE C's CLEAN. OKAY?

RELAX, CAN'T YOU?
IT'S SIMPLE. THIS IS A RETAINER. YOU DON'T DO A THING FOR IT. NOTHING IS WHAT YOU DO. IF YOU KEEP DOING NOTHING FOR A REASONABLE LENGTH OF TIME YOU GET THE SAME AMOUNT LATER ON.
THAT'S SIMPLE, ISN'T IT?

AND WHO AM I DOING THIS NOTHING FOR?
ME. JOSEPH P. TOAD. BUSINESS REPRESENTATIVE, YOU MIGHT CALL ME. JUST A GUY THAT WANTS TO HELP OUT A GUY THAT DON'T WANT TO MAKE TROUBLE FOR A GUY.
AND WHO'S THE BLONDE?

MAYBE YOU'RE INTO THIS TOO FAR ALREADY.
EVER HEARD OF SHERRY BALLOU?
NOPE.
SHERIDAN BALLOU, INCORPORATED, THE BIG HOLLYWOOD AGENT?
MAYBE YOU OUGHT TO LOOK HIM UP SOMETIME.
IS HE HER AGENT?
HE MIGHT BE.
I SUPPOSE YOU REALIZE THAT WE'RE JUST A COUPLE OF BIT PLAYERS, MISTER MARLOWE. THAT'S ALL. JUST A COUPLE OF BIT PLAYERS.
SOMEBODY WANTED TO FIND OUT A LITTLE SOMETHING ABOUT YOU. IT SEEMED THE SIMPLEST WAY TO DO IT.
NOW I'M NOT SO SURE YOU CAN KEEP THE DOUGH. COME ON, ALFRED.

Alfred's eyes crawled sideways watching him. Then jerked to the money on the desk.
Dartingly as an eel he reached for the money, and it disappeared into his pocket.
He gave me a smooth cool empty grin, nodded and moved away, apparently not realizing for a moment that I was holding a gun...

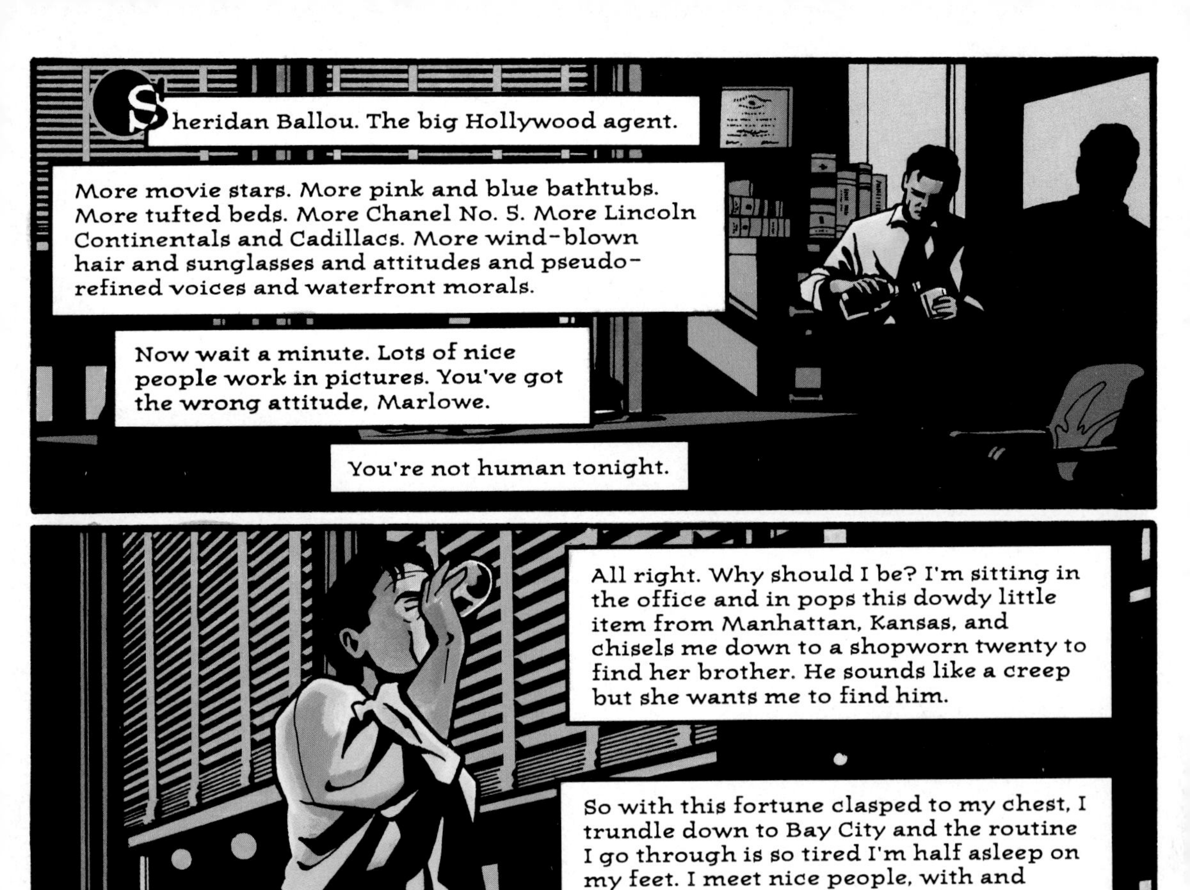

Then she comes in and takes the twenty away from me and gives me a kiss and gives it back to me because I didn't do a full day's work.

So I go see Dr. Hambleton, retired (and how) optometrist from El Centro, and meet again the new style in neckwear. And I don't tell the cops. I just frisk the customer's toupee and put on an act.

Why? Who am I cutting my throat for this time? A blonde with sexy eyes and too many door keys? A girl from Manhattan, Kansas?

All I know is that something isn't what it seems and the old tired but always reliable hunch tells me that if the hand is played the way it is dealt the wrong person is going to lose the pot.

Is that my business? Do I know? Did I ever know? Let's not go into that.

You're not human tonight, Marlowe.

When the phone started ringing I let it ring. I had had enough for one day.
It could have been the Queen of Sheba with her cellophane pajamas on— I was too tired to bother.

3
ABC
2
1
627

No use. I had to go back. Instinct was stronger than weariness.
OH MISTER MARLOWE. I'VE BEEN TRYING TO GET YOU FOR THE LONGEST TIME.
I'VE HEARD FROM ORRIN.

...YOU'RE A NICE LITTLE LIAR. TRY AGAIN SOMETIME WHEN I'M NOT SO TIRED.
VERY WELL, MISTER MARLOWE. I'M READY TO CALL THE POLICE.
BUT I DON'T THINK YOU'LL LIKE IT AT ALL.
MURDER IS A VERY NASTY WORD, DON'T YOU THINK?...

COME ON UP. I'LL WAIT...

She came in briskly enough this time.
There was one of those thin little, bright little smiles on her face.
...SO, ABOUT THIS MURDER. ANYBODY I KNOW? I CAN SEE YOU'RE NOT MURDERED--YET.
PLEASE DON'T BE UNNECESSARILY HORRID. YOU DOUBTED ME OVER THE TELEPHONE SO I HAD TO CONVINCE YOU.
OKAY. SO YOU CONVINCED ME. WHO WAS MURDERED?
THAT DISGUSTING MAN FROM THE ROOMING HOUSE. MISTER-MISTER- I FORGET HIS NAME.
LOOK ORFAMAY, I'M NOT ASKING YOU HOW YOU KNOW ALL THIS. OR RATHER HOW ORRIN KNOWS IT ALL. OR IF HE DOES KNOW IT.
YOU'VE FOUND HIM. THAT'S WHAT YOU WANTED ME TO DO. OR HE'S FOUND YOU, WHICH COMES TO THE SAME THING.

IT'S NOT THE SAME THING. I HAVEN'T REALLY FOUND HIM.
HE WOULDN'T TELL ME WHERE HE WAS LIVING. I DON'T KNOW WHY. HE WOULDN'T TELL ME ANYTHING, REALLY.
JUST ABOUT MURDERS. TRIFLES LIKE THAT.
IT WAS ALL A LIE. EVERYTHING I TOLD YOU WAS A LIE. HE DIDN'T CALL ME UP. I-I DON'T KNOW ANYTHING.
I-I JUST SAID THAT TO SCARE YOU. I DON'T REALLY MEAN ANYBODY WAS MURDERED. YOU SOUNDED SO COLD AND DISTANT.

TAKE THIS MONEY AWAY. ENDOW A HOSPITAL OR A RESEARCH LABORATORY WITH IT. IT MAKES ME NERVOUS HAVING IT AROUND.
BUT YOU WILL FIND ORRIN FOR ME, WON'T YOU?
YEAH, I'LL FIND HIM FOR YOU, IF HE'S STILL ALIVE.

AND FOR FREE. NOT A DIME OF EXPENSE INVOLVED. I ONLY ASK ONE THING.
WHO WAS THE BLACK SHEEP IN YOUR FAMILY?

YOU SAID ORRIN WASN'T THE BLACK SHEEP IN YOUR FAMILY. REMEMBER? WITH A VERY PECULIAR EMPHASIS.
AND WHEN YOU MENTIONED YOUR SISTER LEILA, YOU PASSED ON PRETTY QUICKLY.

I-I DON'T REMEMBER SAYING ANYTHING LIKE THAT.
SO I WAS WONDERING, WHAT NAME DOES YOUR SISTER LEILA USE IN PICTURES?

PICTURES? WHY I NEVER SAID--

YOU LEAVE MY SISTER LEILA OUT OF YOUR DIRTY REMARKS!
MIND YOUR OWN BUSINESS ABOUT MY SISTER LEILA!

I HATE YOU!

A very strange girl.
BAY CITY
CAMERA SHOP
449 Idaho St.
Bay City
8 Enlarged Prints from Negative
Very strange indeed...

By eight forty-five the next morning I had already chewed my way through the Los Angeles paper, which contained no item about ice picks or the Van Nuys or any other hotel. Not even "Mysterious Death in Downtown Hotel," with no names or weapons specified.
Bay City Camera Shop
CLUB
DEWEY HOTEL
HOTEL
FORD
The Bay City NEWS wasn't too busy to write up a murder, though.

They put it on the first page, right next to the price of meat.
A GRAND
Gift
ANYTIME

Local man found sta
in Idaho street rooming
investigation: "It's a tough case, but we'll crack it."
AH. HERE WE ARE, MISTER HICKS...

...EIGHT ENLARGED PRINTS FROM YOUR NEGATIVE.
THANKS.

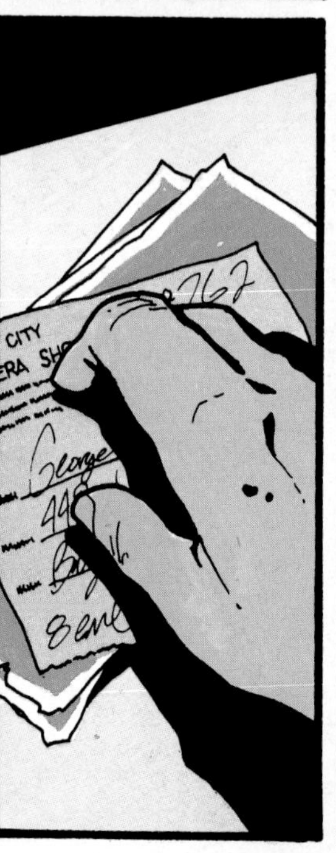
CITY
ERA SH
George

IT IS MISTER HICKS, ISN'T IT...?

I went out and sat in my car and looked over the catch.
DEWEY
HOTEL
HOTEL
The prints showed a couple sitting in a booth in a restaurant. The tablecloth was covered with tiny figures of dancing couples.
That made the restaurant "The Dancers."

The girl was Mavis Weld. The man I didn't recognize. There was no reason why I should.
I figured it must have been a hidden camera trick. It wasn't too hard for me to guess who had taken the picture.
Mr. Orrin P. Quest must have moved fast and smooth to get out of there with his face still on the front of his head.

Hollywood Citizen-News
Light heavyweight
contender succumbs
to ring injuries

I went back to the office and made a few phone calls, then drove down the strip to the offices of Sheridan Ballou, Incorporated.
You can live a long time in Hollywood without ever seeing the part they use in the pictures.
SHERIDAN BALLOU
PRIVATE
THE GIRL IS A CLIENT OF MINE, OF COURSE. THAT FELLOW THAT'S WITH HER IS THE CHAP THAT OWNS "THE DANCERS." NAME OF STEELGRAVE.

BUT IT NEEDS A LITTLE EXPLANATION, DOESN'T IT, MISTER MARLOWE?
ALL I SEE IS TWO PEOPLE HAVING LUNCH IN A PUBLIC PLACE ON A CERTAIN DATE. HARDLY DISASTROUS TO THE REPUTATION OF MY CLIENT.
WHAT WERE YOU THINKING OF ASKING?

YOU DON'T WANT TO BUY ANYTHING, MISTER BALLOU. I COULD HAVE HAD ANOTHER NEGATIVE MADE.
IF THAT SNAP IS EVIDENCE OF ANYTHING, YOU COULD NEVER KNOW YOU HAD SUPPRESSED IT.

THAT'S NOT MUCH OF A SALES PITCH, FOR A BLACKMAILER.

SHE'S CLOSE TO THE BIG MONEY. THAT PICTURE WOULD STOP HER COLD, IF I WERE TO SHOW IT TO THE JOHNS DOWNTOWN.

WHY WOULD THE *POLICE* BE INTER-ESTED?

I'D FIRST HAVE TO CONNECT IT UP WITH SOMETHING THEY'RE WORKING ON--
--SOMETHING THAT HAPPENED AT THE VAN NUYS HOTEL YESTERDAY AFTERNOON.
I'D CONNECT IT UP THROUGH MAVIS WELD-- WHO WON'T TALK TO ME.

YES, SHE *WARNED* ME ABOUT YOU.
TOLD ME ABOUT IT LAST NIGHT.
SAID A PRIVATE DETECTIVE NAMED MARLOWE HAD TRIED TO FORCE HER TO *HIRE* HIM, ON THE GROUNDS THAT SHE WAS SEEN IN A DOWN-TOWN HOTEL *INCONVENIENTLY* CLOSE TO WHERE A *MURDER* WAS COMMITTED.

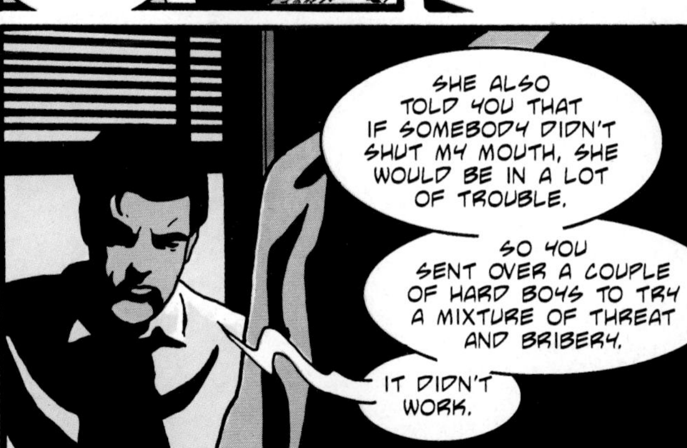
SHE ALSO TOLD YOU THAT IF SOMEBODY DIDN'T SHUT MY MOUTH, SHE WOULD BE IN A LOT OF TROUBLE.
SO YOU SENT OVER A COUPLE OF HARD BOYS TO TRY A MIXTURE OF THREAT AND BRIBERY.
IT DIDN'T WORK.

YOU AMUSE THE *HELL* OUT OF ME, MARLOWE. *REALLY* YOU DO. YOU'RE SO *TRANSPARENT*.
YOU'RE TRYING TO USE *ME* FOR A *SHOVEL* TO DIG YOURSELF OUT OF A JAM.

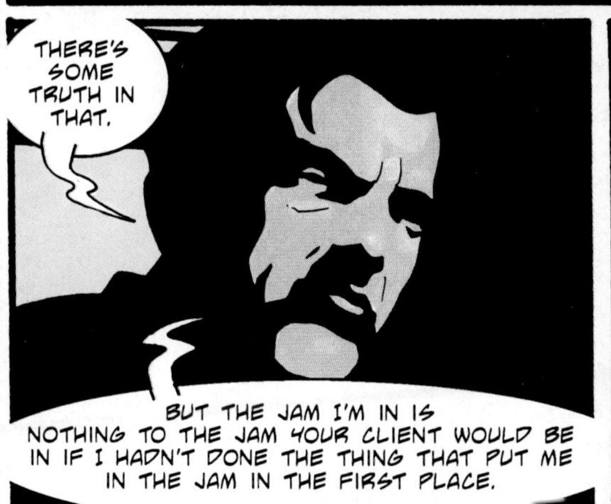
THERE'S SOME TRUTH IN THAT.
BUT THE JAM I'M IN IS NOTHING TO THE JAM YOUR CLIENT WOULD BE IN IF I HADN'T DONE THE THING THAT PUT ME IN THE JAM IN THE FIRST PLACE.

THE MAN WHO TOOK THAT PHOTO IS MISSING AND CAN'T BE FOUND. HE'S PROBABLY DEAD.
TWO OTHER MEN WHO LIVED AT THE SAME ADDRESS ARE DEAD. ONE OF THEM WAS TRYING TO PEDDLE THOSE PICTURES JUST BEFORE HE GOT DEAD.

SHE WENT TO HIS HOTEL ROOM TO TAKE DELIVERY. SO DID WHOEVER KILLED HIM. SHE DIDN'T GET THE DELIVERY AND NEITHER DID THE KILLER.
THEY DIDN'T KNOW WHERE TO LOOK.
AND YOU DID?
I WAS LUCKY. I'D SEEN HIM WITHOUT HIS TOUPÉE.

SHE WANTED THAT PICTURE. GETTING IT WAS WORTH AN AWFUL CHANCE.
WHY?
IT'S JUST TWO PEOPLE HAVING LUNCH ON A CERTAIN DAY.

BUT I DID SOME CHECKING WITH A FRIEND OF MINE AT THE CITIZEN-NEWS. GOT THE DATE ON THAT NEWSPAPER.

THAT PHOTO WAS SNAPPED THE DAY MOE STEIN WAS SHOT TO DEATH ON FRANKLIN AVENUE.
THE DAY A CHARACTER NAMED STEEL-GRAVE...
...THE MAN IN THAT PICTURE, WAS SUPPOSED TO BE IN JAIL BECAUSE THE COPS GOT A TIP HE WAS A CLEVELAND REDHOT NAMED WEEPY MOYER.

THAT'S WHAT THE RECORD SHOWS. BUT THE PHOTO SAYS HE WAS OUT OF JAIL.
AND SHE KNOWS IT.
YOU DON'T REALLY WANT THE COPS TO HAVE THAT PICTURE, DO YOU? WIN, LOSE OR DRAW, THEY'D CRUCIFY HER.
SHE'D BE A GANGSTER'S GIRL IN THE PUBLIC MIND. AND AS FAR AS YOUR BUSINESS IS CONCERNED, SHE'D BE DEFINITELY AND COMPLETELY THROUGH.

WHAT DO YOU REALLY WANT, MARLOWE...?

"YOU THINK I DON'T KNOW MY LINES?
Paramount Pictures
"WELL, IT'S JUST POSSIBLE THAT I'M NOT USED TO PLAYING IN FRONT OF A BACK PROJECTION SCREEN THAT HAS A HABIT OF RUNNING OUT OF FILM ONLY IN THE MIDDLE OF A TAKE."
"LOOK, DICK..."

...IF YOU COULD JUST TAKE THE SCENE A LITTLE FASTER--
HUH. IF I COULD TAKE IT A LITTLE FASTER.
PERHAPS MISS WELD COULD BE PREVAILED UPON TO CLIMB ABOARD THIS SET IN LESS TIME THAN IT WOULD TAKE TO BUILD THE DAMN THING.

WELD'S TIMING IS JUST RIGHT.
I HAD THE IMPRESSION SHE COULD SPEED IT UP A TRIFLE. IT COULD BE BETTER.

IF IT WAS ANY BETTER, DARLING, SOMEBODY MIGHT CALL IT ACTING. YOU WOULDN'T WANT THAT TO HAPPEN IN YOUR PICTURE, WOULD YOU?

ALL RIGHT, ALL RIGHT. BREAK FOR LUNCH EVERYBODY.
WE'LL GET THIS TAKE THIS AFTERNOON.

SO, MISS WELD, DO WE TAKE UP WHERE WE LEFT OFF...

...OR HAVE A NEW DEAL WITH A CLEAN DECK?

SOME-BODY LET YOU IN HERE.
WHO? WHY? THAT TAKES EXPLAINING.

I'M WORKING FOR YOU. I'VE BEEN PAID A RETAINER AND BALLOU HAS THE RECEIPT.
HOW VERY THOUGHTFUL.
AND SUPPOSE I DON'T WANT YOU TO WORK FOR ME? WHATEVER YOUR WORK IS.

ALL RIGHT. BE FANCY.

Hollywood Citizen-News

WELL?
I HAVE THE NEGATIVE AND SOME OTHER PRINTS.
YOU WOULD HAVE HAD THEM, IF YOU HAD HAD SOME MORE TIME AND KNOWN WHERE TO LOOK.

...BETTER COME ALONG TO MY DRESSING ROOM, MARLOWE.

...THERE'S NOT A LOT TO TELL. STEELGRAVE IS A MAN I'VE KNOWN FOR YEARS. AND *LIKED*.
HE OWNS THINGS. A RESTAURANT OR TWO.

WHERE HE COMES FROM--*THAT* I DON'T KNOW.
BUT YOU KNOW HIM VERY WELL.

WHY DON'T YOU JUST ASK ME IF I *SLEEP* WITH HIM?

I DON'T ASK THOSE KINDS OF QUESTIONS.

MISS GONZALES WOULD BE GLAD TO TELL YOU.
THE HELL WITH HER.
ABOUT STEELGRAVE--HAS HE EVER BEEN IN TROUBLE?
DON'T BE *RIDICULOUS*. THE MAN IS WORTH A COUPLE OF MILLION DOLLARS.

HOW DID HE GET IT?
HOW WOULD I KNOW?

ALL RIGHT. YOU WOULDN'T.

Her hand lay on the table. I touched the back of it with a fingertip.
She drew away from me and tightened the hand into a fist.

I REALLY DO HAVE TO EAT SOMETHING, MARLOWE. I'M WORKING THIS AFTERNOON.
YOU WOULDN'T WANT ME TO COLLAPSE ON THE SET, WOULD YOU?
ONLY STARS DO THAT.
OKAY, I'LL LEAVE. DON'T FORGET I'M WORKING FOR YOU. I WOULDN'T BE IF I THOUGHT YOU'D KILLED ANYBODY. BUT YOU WERE THERE. YOU TOOK A BIG CHANCE. THERE WAS SOMETHING YOU WANTED VERY BADLY.

IT COULD HARDLY HAVE BEEN THIS PICTURE.

THAT SNAP IS AS FULL OF MOTIVE AS THE OCEAN IS FULL OF SALT.
AS LONG AS THE COPS DON'T FIND IT I HAVE A LICENSE. AND AS LONG AS SOMEBODY ELSE DOESN'T FIND IT I DON'T HAVE AN ICE PICK IN THE BACK OF MY NECK.

WOULD YOU SAY I WAS IN AN OVERPAID PROFESSION?

There was the usual coming and going in the corridor outside my office, and as I walked through the musty silence there was the usual feeling of having been dropped down a well dried up twenty years ago to which no one would come back ever.
The smell of old dust hung in the air as flat and stale as a football interview.

Inside it was the same dead air, the same dust along the veneer, the same broken promise of a life of ease.

The phone sounded as if it had been ringing for some time.

It was high time I heard from her again.
THIS TIME I REALLY MEAN IT.
I LIED BEFORE. I'M NOT LYING NOW.
GO ON.
I REALLY HAVE HEARD FROM ORRIN.
WE'VE BEEN THROUGH THAT ROUTINE. YOU'RE FORGETFUL FOR YOUR AGE.
PLEASE THIS IS VERY SERIOUS. HE GOT MY LETTER. HE WENT TO THE POST OFFICE AND ASKED FOR HIS MAIL.
HE KNEW WHERE I'D BE STAYING AND CALLED ME FROM BAY CITY. HE'S STAYING WITH A DOCTOR HE GOT TO KNOW DOWN THERE. DOING SOME KIND OF WORK FOR HIM.

HE'S AFRAID TO LEAVE THE HOUSE. PLEASE GO DOWN THERE AND SEE IF YOU CAN HELP HIM.
DOCTOR HAVE A NAME?
YES. A FUNNY NAME.

DOCTOR VINCENT LAGARDIE.

"I DON'T KNOW ANYONE NAMED ORRIN QUEST, MISTER MARLOWE.
"I CAN'T IMAGINE ANY REASON IN THE WORLD WHY A PERSON OF THAT NAME SHOULD SAY HE WAS IN MY HOUSE."
DR. VINCENT LAGARDIE
NEUROLOGY ASSOCIATES
HIDING OUT.
FROM WHAT?
FROM SOME GUYS THAT MIGHT WANT TO STICK AN ICE PICK IN THE BACK OF HIS NECK.
IT WAS YOU WHO SENT THE POLICE HERE, WASN'T IT?
IT WAS YOU WHO CALLED UP AND REPORTED CLAUSEN'S DEATH. IT WAS YOU WHO CALLED ME AND ASKED IF I KNEW CLAUSEN.
I SAID I DID NOT.
YEAH, I KNOW YOU DID.
I DIDN'T QUITE BELIEVE YOU.
THE POLICE HAVE BEEN HERE, MISTER MARLOWE. A CERTAIN LIEUTENANT MAGLASHAN. SHALL I CALL HIM?
GO AHEAD, CALL HIM. BOTH OF US ARE GOING TO BE IN THE CLINK BEFORE NIGHTFALL, ANYWAY.
YOU, BECAUSE CLAUSEN KNEW YOU BY YOUR FIRST NAME. AND YOU MAY HAVE BEEN THE LAST MAN HE TALKED TO.
ME, BECAUSE I'VE BEEN DOING ALL THE THINGS A P.I. NEVER GETS AWAY WITH. HIDING EVIDENCE, HIDING INFORMATION.
OH, I'M THROUGH. BUT THERE'S A WILD PERFUME IN THE AIR THIS AFTERNOON. I DON'T SEEM TO CARE, OR I'M IN LOVE.
I JUST DON'T SEEM TO CARE.

WOMEN CAN WEAKEN A MAN TERRIBLY, CAN THEY NOT?

CLAUSEN.

A HOPELESS ALCOHOLIC. THEY DRINK AND THEY DON'T EAT. AND LITTLE BY LITTLE THE VITAMIN DEFICIENCY BRINGS ON THE SYMPTOMS OF DELIRIUM.
THERE IS ONLY ONE THING TO DO FOR THEM. NEEDLES AND MORE NEEDLES. IT MAKES ME FEEL DIRTY.

I AM A GRADUATE OF THE SORBONNE. BUT I PRACTICE AMONG DIRTY LITTLE PEOPLE IN A DIRTY LITTLE TOWN.
WHY?
BECAUSE OF SOMETHING THAT HAPPENED YEARS AGO-- IN ANOTHER CITY. DON'T ASK ME TOO MUCH, MISTER MARLOWE.
WOULD YOU CARE FOR A CIGARETTE?

THANKS.
WERE YOU BY ANY CHANCE A MEDIC FOR THE GANG BOYS IN SOME HOT EASTERN CITY?
AS FOR INSTANCE, CLEVELAND?

A VERY WILD SUGGESTION, MY FRIEND.

WILD AS HELL. THEY HAVE A WHOLE ROOMFUL OF DIRECTORIES OVER AT THE TELEPHONE OFFICE. FROM ALL OVER THE COUNTRY.
I CHECKED YOU UP.
YOU WOULD HAVE CHANGED YOUR NAME, BUT YOU COULDN'T AND KEEP YOUR LICENSE.

A FELLOW LIKE ME WITH VERY LIMITED BRAINS TENDS TO FIT THE THINGS HE KNOWS INTO A PATTERN.
IT GOES LIKE THIS, IF YOU WANT TO LISTEN.

"YOU KNEW CLAUSEN. CLAUSEN WAS KILLED VERY SKILLFULLY WITH AN ICE PICK, KILLED WHILE I WAS IN THE HOUSE, UPSTAIRS TALKING TO A GRIFTER NAMED HICKS.
"HICKS MOVED OUT FAST TAKING A PAGE OF THE REGISTER WITH HIM, THE PAGE THAT HAD ORRIN QUEST'S NAME ON IT.

"LATER THAT AFTERNOON HICKS WAS KILLED WITH AN ICE PICK IN L.A.
"HIS ROOM HAD BEEN SEARCHED. THERE WAS A WOMAN THERE WHO HAD COME TO BUY SOMETHING FROM HIM. SHE DIDN'T GET IT.
"I HAD MORE TIME TO SEARCH FOR IT. I DID GET IT.
"PRESUMPTION A: CLAUSEN AND HICKS KILLED BY THE SAME PERSON, NOT NECESSARILY FOR SAME REASON. ANY GOOD SO FAR?"
"NOT OF THE SLIGHTEST INTEREST TO ME."

"BUT YOU ARE LISTENING.
"OKAY. NOW WHAT DID I FIND? A PHOTO OF A MOVIE QUEEN AND AN EX-CLEVELAND GANGSTER, MAYBE ON A PARTICULAR DAY.
"DAY WHEN THE EX-GANGSTER WAS SUPPOSED TO BE IN HOCK AT THE COUNTY JAIL, ALSO DAY WHEN EX-GANGSTER'S ONETIME SIDEKICK WAS SHOT DEAD ON FRANKLIN AVENUE IN L.A.

"WHY WAS HE IN HOCK? TIP-OFF THAT HE WAS WHO HE WAS. WHO GAVE HIM THE TIP?
"THE GUY GAVE IT TO THEM HIMSELF, BECAUSE HIS EX-PARTNER WAS BEING TROUBLESOME AND HAD TO BE RUBBED OUT, AND BEING IN JAIL WAS A FIRST-CLASS ALIBI.
"PHOTO THEREFORE STRONG BLACKMAIL MATERIAL."
BOGART
ASTOR
Falcon

ALL FANTASTIC. UTTERLY FANTASTIC.

SURE. IT GETS WORSE.
OKAY, PRESUMPTION B: ORRIN QUEST TOOK THAT PHOTO. HOW?
THE MOVIE QUEEN IS HIS SISTER. STILL UTTERLY FANTASTIC, DOCTOR?

I'LL TIE YOU IN ON IT NOW.
YOU KNEW CLAUSEN, PROFESSIONALLY, YOU SAID. AND IF YOU KNEW CLAUSEN, YOU COULD HAVE KNOWN SOME OF HIS ROOMERS. PARAGRAPH.
PRESUMPTION C: YOU KNEW HICKS OR ORRIN QUEST OR BOTH.
SOMEBODY HAD TO MASTERMIND THIS DEAL, DOCTOR. YOU COULDN'T GO UP AGAINST THE EX-CLEVELAND GANGSTER--LET'S GIVE HIM HIS NAME, STEELGRAVE--YOU COULDN'T GO UP AGAINST STEELGRAVE DIRECTLY. YOU HAD TO WORK THROUGH PAWNS--EXPENDABLE PAWNS.

WELL--ARE WE GETTING ANYWHERE?

PRESUMPTION D, MISTER MARLOWE: YOU ARE AN UNMITIGATED IDIOT.

ADDED TO ALL THE REST, ORRIN'S SISTER CALLS ME UP AND TELLS ME HE IS IN YOUR HOUSE,
THERE ARE A LOT OF WEAK ARGUMENTS, I ADMIT, BUT THEY DO SEEM TO SORT OF FOCUS ON YOU, AND...AND...

His face seemed to fluctuate and become vague, to move far off and come back.
I felt a tightness in my chest.
My mind had slowed to a turtle's gallop.

WHAT'S GOING ON HERE? BEEN DUMB HAVEN'T I?

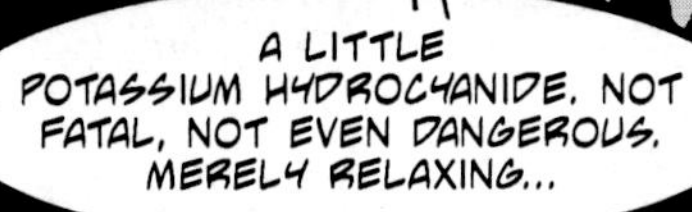
A LITTLE POTASSIUM HYDROCYANIDE. NOT FATAL, NOT EVEN DANGEROUS. MERELY RELAXING...

DR. VINCENT LAGARDIE
NEUROLOGY ASSOCIATES

12
Appointments
Cancelled

DR. LAGARDIE
PRIVATE

My eyelids were as hard to lift as a dead elephant. I decided to open them just the same.
Others had done it, why not me?

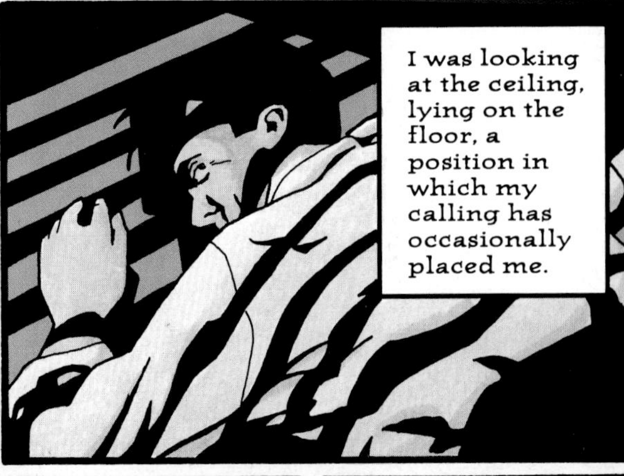
I was looking at the ceiling, lying on the floor, a position in which my calling has occasionally placed me.

How long had I been out?

I got up on my haunches and braced myself and shook my head.
It went into a flat spin.

It spun down about five thousand feet and then I dragged it out and leveled off.
I was as dizzy as a dervish, as weak as a worn-out washer, and as unlikely to succeed as a ballet dancer with a wooden leg.

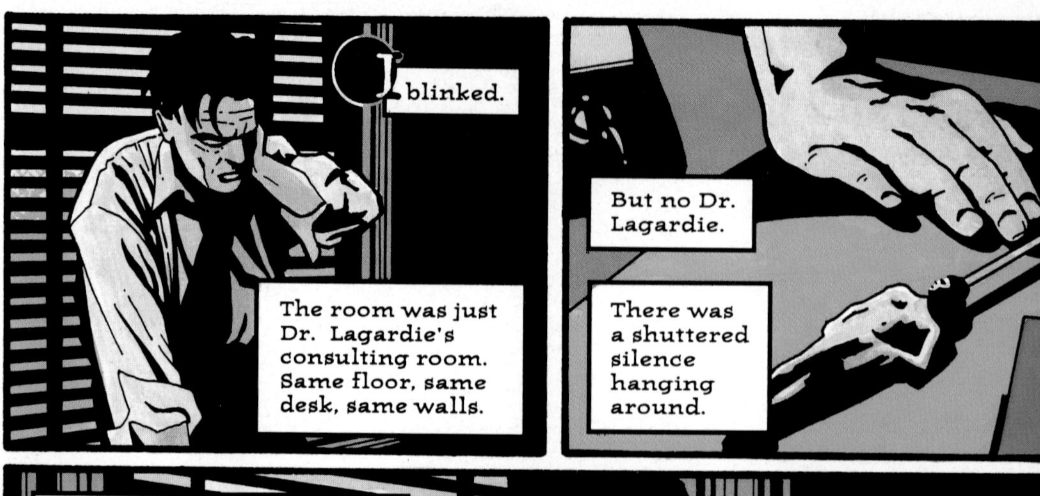
I blinked.
The room was just Dr. Lagardie's consulting room. Same floor, same desk, same walls.
But no Dr. Lagardie.
There was a shuttered silence hanging around.

At the moment I was aware that steps were coming down the hall. Slow, dragging steps with a long pause between each.
They stopped at the door.

Our faces were inches apart. Our breathing met in midair.

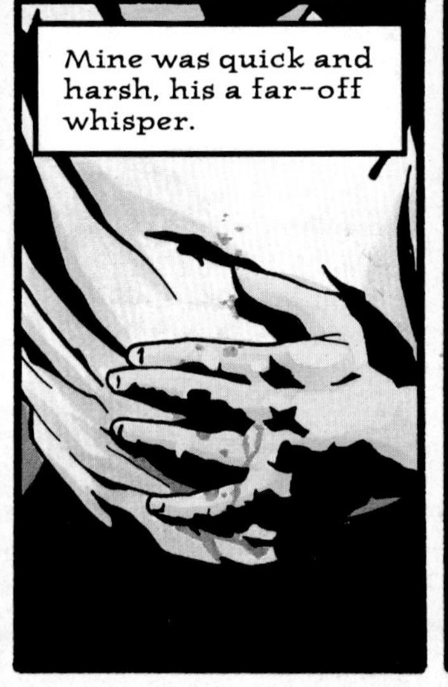
Mine was quick and harsh, his a far-off whisper.

The man's body began to wink up on his legs, and his heels squeaked on the linoleum.

His torso turned in midair, like a swimmer in a wave, and jumped at me.

Something thumped to the floor and rattled to a stop.

His teeth clicked and I thought he was going to speak, or try to speak.
But that was the only sound from him.
He had stopped breathing.
I looked down at the ice pick he had dropped. The point was filed down not more than three inches long.
Compliments of CRUMSEN HARDWARE Co
It was very sharp.
Something happened to his face and behind his face, the smoothing out, the going back over the years to the age of innocence.
All of which was very silly, because I knew damn well, if I ever knew anything at all,...
...that Orrin Quest had not been that kind of boy...

I wiped off everything with my handkerchief and followed the trail of blood through the silent and waiting house.
The trail led me back and across to a room furnished like a den. A metallic glitter near the leg of the studio couch turned out to be a used shell from an automatic—.32 caliber. I found another under the desk. I put them in my pocket.
In one of the bedrooms I found Orrin Quest's meager wardrobe. Under his shirts was a Leica camera with an F.2 lens.
I left all these things as they were and went back downstairs into the room where the dead man lay indifferent to these trifles. I wiped off a few more doorknobs out of sheer perverseness, hesitated over the phone in the front room, and left without touching it.
The fact that I was still walking around was a pretty good indication that the good Dr. Lagardie hadn't killed anybody.

Besides, Orfamay Quest had a right to know first, law or no law.
And I was far outside the law already.
I would have to tell her a harder thing than she dreamed of, and after a while she would go and I would never see her again.

Amigo, please call me at my apartment—
Chateau Bercy.
Most urgent.
Must see you.
Delores Gonzales
PAST DUE

Orfamay might be in there already, waiting.
615

'ALLO, AMIGO. I WAITED A LONG TIME. YOU DID NOT CALL.

THE ACCENT'S A BIT THICK THIS EVENING.
I AM *NOT* IN AN AMUSING MOOD TONIGHT, AMIGO.
YOU DON'T HAVE TO AMUSE ME. I AMUSE MYSELF. YOU ALWAYS WEAR BLACK?
BUT YES. IT IS MORE EXCITING WHEN I TAKE MY CLOTHES OFF.

DO YOU EVER THINK OF ANYTHING BUT ONE THING?
THIS IS HOW I CATCH FOOLS, AMIGO. SOME FOOLS ARE USEFUL AND GENEROUS. OCCASIONALLY ONE IS DANGEROUS.

IF YOU'RE WAITING FOR ME TO LET ON I KNOW WHO A CERTAIN PARTY IS--OKAY, I KNOW WHO HE IS.
I PROBABLY CAN'T PROVE IT. THE COPS COULDN'T.

THE COPS DO NOT ALWAYS TELL ALL THEY KNOW. THEY DO NOT ALWAYS PROVE ALL THEY CAN PROVE.

I SUPPOSE YOU KNOW HE WAS IN JAIL FOR TEN DAYS LAST FEBRUARY.
YES.

HE WAS MY BOYFRIEND ALSO.

BELIEVE IT OR NOT, MISS GONZALES, I'M NOT INTERESTED IN YOUR LOVE LIFE.
I ASSUME IT COVERS A WIDE FIELD--ALL THE WAY FROM STEIN TO STEELGRAVE.
STEIN? WHO IS STEIN?

A CLEVELAND HOT SHOT THAT GOT HIMSELF GUNNED IN FRONT OF YOUR APARTMENT HOUSE LAST FEBRUARY.
REPORTS SAY IT HAPPENED TWO BLOCKS AWAY.

I LIKE IT BETTER THAT IT HAPPENED RIGHT IN FRONT. AND YOU WERE LOOKING OUT OF THE WINDOW AND SAW IT HAPPEN.
AND DARNED IF THE KILLER WASN'T OLD MAN STEELGRAVE.

YOU LIKE IT BETTER THAT WAY.

WE MAKE MORE MONEY THAT WAY.

BUT STEELGRAVE WAS IN JAIL.
AND EVEN IF HE WAS NOT IN JAIL--EVEN IF, FOR EXAMPLE, I HAPPENED TO BE FRIENDLY WITH A CERTAIN DOCTOR CHALMERS WHO WAS COUNTY JAIL PHYSICIAN AT THE TIME AND HE TOLD ME, IN AN INTIMATE MOMENT, THAT HE HAD GIVEN STEELGRAVE A PASS TO GO TO THE DENTIST--
--WITH A GUARD OF COURSE, BUT THE GUARD WAS A REASONABLE MAN--ON THE VERY DAY STEIN WAS SHOT--
--EVEN IF THIS HAPPENED TO BE TRUE, WOULD IT NOT BE A VERY POOR WAY TO USE THE INFORMATION BY BLACKMAILING STEELGRAVE?

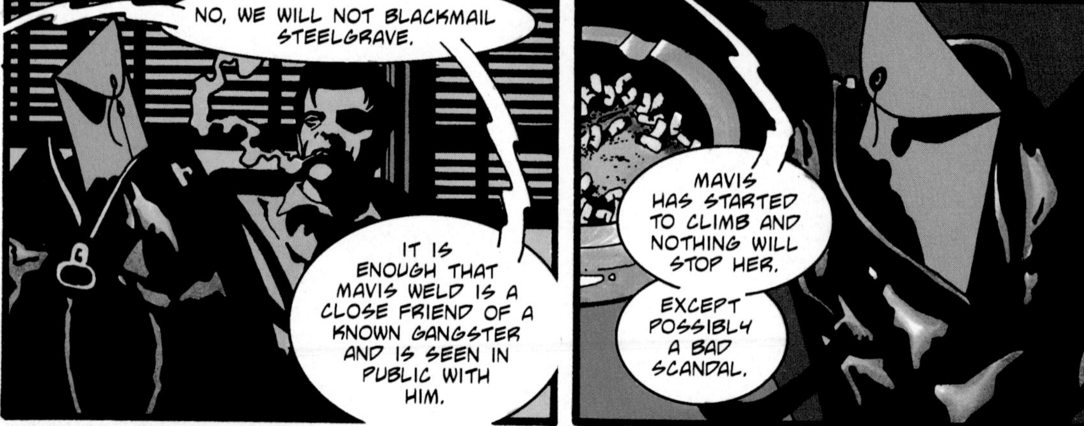
NO, WE WILL NOT BLACKMAIL STEELGRAVE.
IT IS ENOUGH THAT MAVIS WELD IS A CLOSE FRIEND OF A KNOWN GANGSTER AND IS SEEN IN PUBLIC WITH HIM.
MAVIS HAS STARTED TO CLIMB AND NOTHING WILL STOP HER.
EXCEPT POSSIBLY A BAD SCANDAL.

WE'D HAVE TO PROVE STEELGRAVE WAS A KNOWN GANGSTER. WE CAN'T.
AND EVEN IF WE COULD, WHAT'S HE DOING ALL THE TIME WE'RE PUTTING THE BITE ON WELD?

DOES HE HAVE TO KNOW? I HARDLY THINK SHE WOULD TELL HIM.
BUT THAT WOULD NOT MATTER TO *US*--IF WE HAD OUR PROOF.

...I MIGHT HAPPEN TO BE UNDER SOME OBLIGATION TO MISS WELD. EVER THINK OF THAT?
AND IF THAT WAS SO, DON'T YOU THINK IT WAS ABOUT TIME YOU GOT THE HELL OUT OF MY OFFICE?

She picked up her hat and started to get up.

I scooped the envelope from the bag before she could change direction.

She made a spitting sound.

WHERE DID YOU GET THIS?
FROM MAVIS WELD'S PURSE IN MAVIS WELD'S DRESSING ROOM. WHILE SHE WAS ON THE SET.

I WONDER WHERE SHE GOT IT.

FROM YOU.

NONSENSE. WHERE WOULD I GET IT?

GIVE IT BACK TO ME!
IF YOU DO NOT--

I'LL GIVE IT BACK TO MISS WELD.
AND I HATE TO TELL YOU THIS, MISS GONZALES, BUT I'D NEVER GET ANYWHERE AS A BLACKMAILER. I JUST DON'T HAVE THE ENGAGING PERSONALITY.

VERY WELL. IT IS MY MISTAKE. I CAN SEE THAT YOU ARE JUST ANOTHER DUMB PRIVATE EYE.
THIS SHABBY LITTLE OFFICE-- IT OUGHT TO TELL ME WHAT SORT OF *IDIOT* YOU ARE.

IT DOES.

The way she went out hadn't been learned in business college.
She went on down the hall without looking back.

Then I turned and started back towards my desk and the phone rang.
It was Christy French downtown.

MARLOWE? WE'D LIKE TO SEE YOU DOWN AT HEAD-QUARTERS.
RIGHT AWAY?
IF NOT SOONER.

You'd think she would have called by now.

The building seemed quiet this afternoon.
After a while it would be silent and then the madonna of the dark-grey mop would come shuffling along the hall, trying doorknobs.

When the phone rang I nearly took the door off its hinges getting back to it.
It was her voice all right, but it had a tone I had never heard before.
I knew before she said three words.
YOU DON'T HAVE TO TELL ME ANYTHING. I WENT DOWN THERE.
...YOU WENT DOWN THERE...
I JUST HAD A FEELING, HE BEING MY BROTHER AND ALL.
I RANG THE BELL, AND NOBODY ANSWERED THE DOOR. THAT SEEMED FUNNY. MAYBE I'M A PSYCHIC OR SOMETHING. ALL OF A SUDDEN I SEEMED TO HAVE TO GET INTO THAT HOUSE, AND I DIDN'T KNOW HOW.
SO I CALLED THE POLICE. I LIED. I TOLD THEM I HEARD SHOTS.
THAT'S ALL RIGHT. I WOULD HAVE CALLED THEM MYSELF AS SOON AS I COULD TELL YOU.

YOU LEFT HIM LYING ON THE FLOOR.
DEAD.
YOU HAD TO, I GUESS.
I HAD MY REASONS. THEY WON'T SOUND TOO GOOD, BUT I HAD THEM.
IT MADE NO DIFFERENCE TO HIM.
OH, YOU HAD YOUR REASONS ALL RIGHT.
WELL, I GUESS YOU'LL HAVE TO TELL THE POLICE YOUR REASONS TOO. I HAD TO TELL THEM ABOUT YOU.
615
PHILIP MARLOWE
IN MY BUSINESS A FELLOW DOES WHAT HE CAN TO PROTECT A CLIENT.
THAT'S WHAT I DID, BUT NOT ENTIRELY FOR YOU.
YOU LEFT HIM LYING ON THE FLOOR DEAD. AND I DON'T CARE WHAT THEY DO TO YOU.
IF THEY PUT YOU IN PRISON, I THINK I WOULD LIKE THAT.

I DID MY BEST FOR YOU.
PERHAPS IF YOU'D GIVEN ME A LITTLE MORE INFORMATION IN THE BEGINNING THEN--

She hung up on me while I was saying it.

You drove off a cliff all right, Marlowe.

Marlowe, Philip
Clausen
Quest

NOW IF YOU'RE IN THE MOOD YOU COULD START AT THE BEGINNING AND GIVE US ALL THE STUFF YOU LEFT OUT YESTERDAY.
DON'T TRY TO SORT IT OUT. JUST LET IT FLOW NATURAL.
A VERY *FULL STATEMENT.* FUN, HUH!
YOU WANT ME TO MAKE A STATEMENT?
AND THIS STATEMENT IS TO BE VOLUNTARY AND WITHOUT COERCION?
SOME GUYS ARE MORE *VOLUNTARY* THAN *OTHERS.*

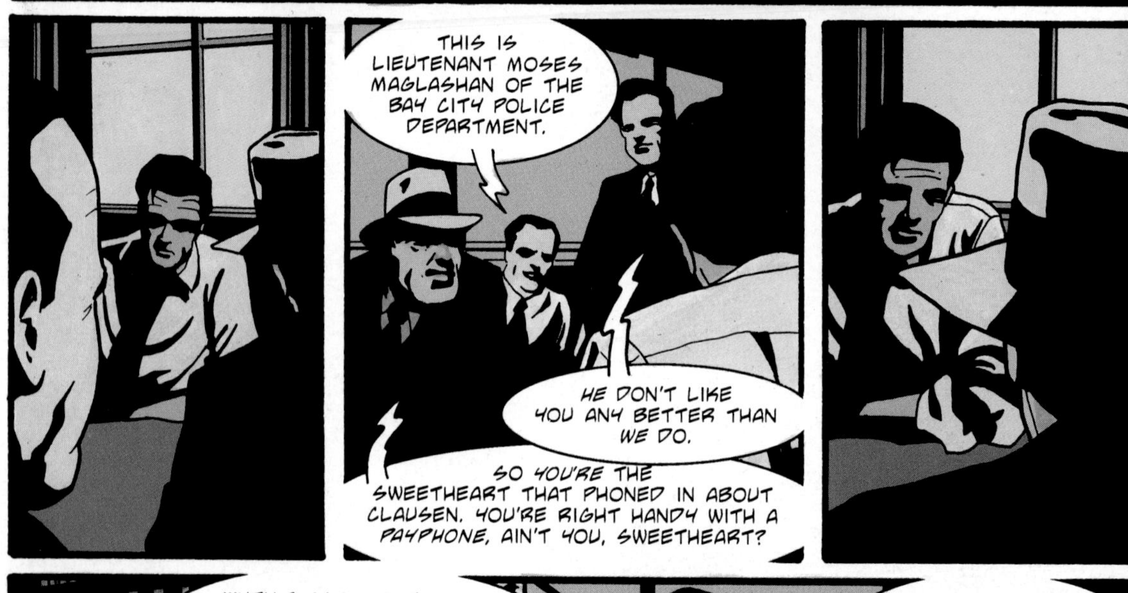
THIS IS LIEUTENANT MOSES MAGLASHAN OF THE BAY CITY POLICE DEPARTMENT.
HE DON'T LIKE YOU ANY BETTER THAN *WE* DO.
SO *YOU'RE* THE SWEETHEART THAT PHONED IN ABOUT CLAUSEN. YOU'RE RIGHT HANDY WITH A *PAYPHONE*, AIN'T YOU, SWEETHEART?

WHEN I ASK A QUESTION I GET ANSWERED. GET THAT, SWEETHEART?
I'M *TALKING* TO YOU, SWEET-HEART.
WHAT MAKES YOU BAY CITY COPS SO *TOUGH?*
YOU PICKLE YOUR *NUTS* IN *SALT WATER* OR SOMETHING?

I CAME DOWN HERE TO GET SOME COOPERATION.
YOU'LL GET COOPERATION.

JUST DON'T TRY TO STEAL THE SCENE WITH THAT NINETEEN-THIRTIES DIALOGUE.
LET'S TAKE OUT A CLEAN SHEET OF PAPER AND PLAY LIKE WE'RE JUST STARTING THIS INVESTIGATION.

ASK THE QUESTIONS. IF YOU DON'T LIKE THE ANSWERS YOU CAN BOOK ME.
IF YOU BOOK ME, I GET TO MAKE A PHONE CALL.

IF WE BOOK YOU.
BUT WE DON'T *HAVE* TO. WE CAN RIDE THE *CIRCUIT* WITH YOU. IT MIGHT TAKE *DAYS*.
AND CANNED CORNBEEF HASH TO EAT.

STRICTLY SPEAKING, IT WOULDN'T BE *LEGAL*, LIKE *YOU* DO A FEW THINGS WHICH *YOU* HADN'T OUGHT TO DO, MAYBE.
WOULD YOU SAY YOU WERE LEGAL IN THIS PICTURE?
NO.

HA!
YOU GOT A *CLIENT* TO PROTECT.

MAYBE.

YOU MEAN YOU *DID* HAVE A CLIENT. SHE *RATTED* ON YOU.
NAME'S ORFAMAY QUEST.

...ALL RIGHT.
YESTERDAY, I WENT DOWN TO BAY CITY. A PLACE ON IDAHO STREET.

"...I WENT THERE LOOKING FOR HER BROTHER.
"HE'D MOVED AWAY, SHE SAID, AND SHE'D COME OUT HERE TO SEE HIM. SHE WAS WORRIED.
"THE MANAGER, CLAUSEN, WAS TOO DRUNK TO TALK SENSE. I LOOKED AT THE REGISTER AND SAW ANOTHER MAN HAD MOVED INTO QUEST'S ROOM. I TALKED TO THIS MAN. HE TOLD ME NOTHING THAT HELPED.
"WHEN I WENT BACK DOWNSTAIRS CLAUSEN WAS DEAD. AN ICE PICK IN THE BACK OF HIS NECK. AND SOMEBODY HAD TORN A PAGE OUT OF THE REGISTER.
"THE PAGE WITH ORRIN QUEST'S NAME ON IT.
"LATER, I REPORTED TO THE CLIENT.
VAN NUYS
"THEN A GUY CALLED ME UP AND ASKED ME OVER TO THE VAN NUYS HOTEL. YOU SAW WHAT HAPPENED THERE. ANOTHER ICE PICK.
"WHAT I DIDN'T TELL YOU WAS THAT HE WAS THE SAME GUY I HAD TALKED TO DOWN ON IDAHO STREET, BUT WITH A DIFFERENT NAME.
Milk
"SO TODAY, THE CLIENT TOLD ME HER BROTHER HAD CALLED HER UP FROM THIS DOCTOR'S HOUSE. DOCTOR LAGARDIE.
"THE BROTHER WAS IN DANGER. I WAS TO HURRY ON DOWN AND TAKE CARE OF HIM. I HURRIED ON DOWN. DOCTOR LAGARDIE ACTED SCARED. THE POLICE HAD BEEN THERE.
"LAGARDIE DENIED KNOWING ANYTHING ABOUT ORRIN QUEST.
"THEN HE SLIPPED ME A DOPED CIGARETTE AND I WENT AWAY FROM THERE FOR A WHILE.
"WHEN I CAME TO I WAS ALONE IN THE HOUSE.
"THEN I WASN'T. ORRIN QUEST, OR WHAT WAS LEFT OF HIM, CAME IN AND DIED.
"WITH HIS LAST OUNCE OF STRENGTH HE TRIED TO STICK ME WITH AN ICE PICK."

WHY WOULD HE WANT TO STICK YOU? YOU WERE HIS *PAL*. YOU WERE THERE TO KEEP HIM *SAFE* FOR HIS SISTER.
I'D NEVER SEEN HIM BEFORE.
IF HE EVER SAW ME, I DIDN'T KNOW IT.
IT COULD HAVE BEEN A BEAUTIFUL FRIENDSHIP.
EXCEPT FOR THE ICE PICK, OF COURSE.

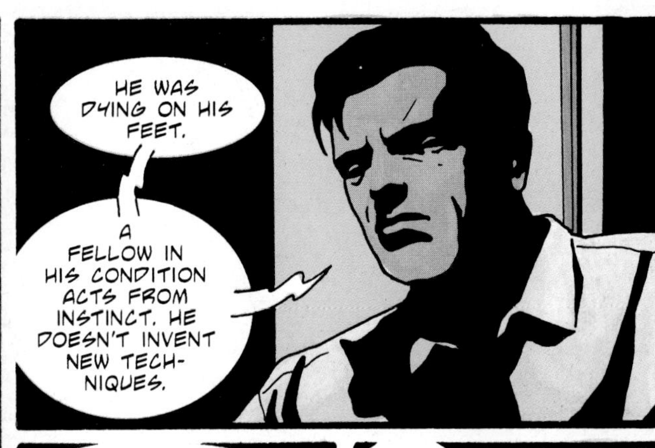
HE WAS DYING ON HIS FEET.
A FELLOW IN HIS CONDITION ACTS FROM INSTINCT. HE DOESN'T INVENT NEW TECH-NIQUES.

SOMEBODY'S A GODDAMN *LIAR* AND IT *AIN'T* ME.

ALL RIGHT, ALL RIGHT.
LET'S NOT BE THEATRICAL.

LET'S HAVE YOUR IDEAS ABOUT ALL THIS, MARLOWE.
AMONG OTHER THINGS CLAUSEN WAS PROBABLY PUSHING REEFERS.

BUT HE WAS LIQUORED TO A POINT WHERE YOU WOULDN'T WANT TO TRUST HIM ANYMORE. THEY DON'T GO FOR THAT IN ORGAN-IZATIONS.
THE MINUTE THEY SMELLED DICK AROUND THE HOUSE CLAUSEN WOULD BE MISSING.
SUPPOSE IT WAS SO, WHAT'S IT GOT TO DO WITH QUEST?

SUPPOSE QUEST TRIED TO PUT THE BITE ON SOMEBODY AND THREATENED TO GO TO THE POLICE?
QUITE POSSIBLY ALL THREE MURDERS ARE CONNECTED WITH THE REEFER GANG.

THAT DON'T JIBE WITH QUEST HAVING THE ICE PICK.
THEY MIGHT BE STANDARD EQUIPMENT AROUND DOCTOR LAGARDIE'S HOUSE.
GET ANYTHING ON HIM?

NOT SO FAR. WHAT DO YOU MAKE OF HIM?
HE DIDN'T KILL ME, PROBABLY HE DIDN'T KILL ANYBODY.
HE USED TO PRACTICE IN CLEVELAND. DOWNTOWN IN A LARGE WAY.

HE MUST HAVE HAD HIS REASONS FOR HIDING OUT IN BAY CITY.
PROBABLY AN *ABORTIONIST.*
I'VE HAD MY *EYE* ON HIM FOR SOME TIME.

WHICH EYE?
PROBABLY THE ONE HE *DIDN'T* HAVE ON *IDAHO STREET.*

YOU BOYS THINK YOU'RE SO GODDAMN *SMART--*
--IT MIGHT INTEREST YOU TO KNOW THAT WE'RE JUST A SMALL TOWN POLICE FORCE.

JUST THE SAME I *LIKE* THAT REEFER ANGLE. IT MIGHT CUT DOWN MY WORK CONSIDERABLY.
I'M LOOKING INTO IT *RIGHT* NOW.

Maglashan marched solidly out of the room.
French looked after him. Beifus did the same. When he was gone, they looked at each other, then turned back to me.
IF YOU WERE GUESSING, MARLOWE, WHAT WOULD YOU GUESS THEY WERE LOOKING FOR IN THAT ROOM AT THE VAN NUYS?
A CLAIM CHECK FOR A SUITCASE FULL OF WEED.
WHEN I TALKED TO HICKS DOWN IN BAY CITY HE WASN'T WEARING HIS MUFF. BUT HE WAS WEARING IT ON THE BED AT THE VAN NUYS. WOULDN'T BE A BAD PLACE TO STASH A CLAIM CHECK.

YOU COULD PIN IT DOWN WITH A PIECE OF SCOTCH TAPE. QUITE AN IDEA.
STILL GUESSING, HOW DID DOCTOR LA-GARDIE COME TO MENTION CLEVELAND TO YOU?

I TOOK THE TROUBLE TO LOOK HIM UP. A DOCTOR CAN'T CHANGE HIS NAME IF HE WANTS TO GO ON PRACTICING.
THE ICE PICK MAKES YOU THINK OF WEEPY MOYER. WEEPY MOYER OPERATED IN CLEVELAND. SUNNY MOE STEIN OPERATED IN CLEVELAND. AND ALWAYS WITH THESE GANGS THERE'S A DOCTOR IN THE BACKGROUND.

PRETTY WILD. PRETTY LOOSE CONNECTION.
WOULD I DO MYSELF ANY GOOD IF I TRIED TO TIGHTEN IT UP?
LET'S BREAK THIS OFF.
THE NEXT MOVE IS UP TO THE D.A. AND IF I KNOW ENDICOTT, IT WILL BE A WEEK FROM TUESDAY BEFORE HE DECIDES HOW TO PLAY IT.

GO ON OUT AND SQUARE THINGS UP. MAGLASHAN BOUGHT YOU A RAIN CHECK.
USE IT.

WOULD IT BE ALL RIGHT IF I DON'T LEAVE TOWN...?

Outside the going home sounds had died away and the neon signs began to glare at one another across the boulevard.
I used to like this town. A long time ago. There were trees along Wilshire Boulevard. Beverly Hills was a country town. Los Angeles was just a big dry sunny place with ugly homes and no style, but goodhearted and peaceful.
Now we get characters like this Steelgrave owning restaurants.
We've got the big money, the sharp-shooters, the percentage workers, the fast-dollar boys, the hoodlums out of New York and Chicago - and Cleveland. The riffraff of a hard-boiled city with no more personality than a paper cup.
GO
STOP
EXTRA
Real cities have something else, some individual bony structure under the muck. Los Angeles has Hollywood —and hates it. It ought to consider itself damn lucky.
Without Hollywood it would be a mail order city. Everything in the catalogue you could get better somewhere else.

The office was empty again.
There was something to be done, but I didn't know what. Whatever it was would be useless.

I was a blank man. I had no face, no meaning, no personality, hardly a name.
I was the page from yesterday's calendar crumpled at the bottom of the waste-basket.

I wished that the telephone would ring. Let there be somebody to call up and plug me into the human race again.
Even a cop. Even a Maglashan. Nobody has to like me.

I was psychic that night. The telephone rang.

AMIGO, THERE IS TROUBLE. BAD TROUBLE.
MAVIS WANTS TO SEE YOU. SHE LIKES YOU. SHE THINKS YOU ARE AN HONEST MAN.
I WILL BE BEFORE YOUR BUILDING IN FIFTEEN MINUTES...

Dolores Gonzales's was a black convertible with a light top.
We headed west, through Beverly Hills and then further on.
The inside of my left arm pressed against the luger in its shoulder harness.
WHY DIDN'T MISS WELD CALL ME HERSELF?
SHE COULDN'T. SHE DID NOT HAVE THE NUMBER AND THERE SEEMED TO BE VERY LITTLE TIME. IT SEEMED TO BE WHILE SOMEONE WAS OUT OF THE ROOM FOR JUST A MOMENT.
YOU ARE BITTER TONIGHT, AMIGO.
I'VE GOT A FEW TROUBLES.
THE ONLY REASON I'M HERE IS THAT I'VE GOT SO MUCH TROUBLE--
--A LITTLE MORE WILL SEEM LIKE ICING.
ALWAYS THE WISECRACK. IT IS A VERY STRANGE MAN.
ALWAYS THE WISECRACK WHERE POSSIBLE.
AND IT IS A VERY ORDINARY GUY WITH ONLY ONE HEAD--WHICH HAS BEEN RATHER HARSHLY USED AT TIMES. THE TIMES USUALLY STARTED OUT LIKE THIS.
WHAT KIND OF TROUBLE IS MISS WELD IN?
I DO NOT KNOW. SHE JUST SAID IT WAS TROUBLE AND SHE WAS MUCH AFRAID AND SHE NEEDED YOU.
YOU OUGHT TO BE ABLE TO THINK UP A BETTER STORY THAN THAT.
I WOULD NOT HURT A HAIR OF MAVIS WELD'S HEAD.
I DO NOT QUITE EXPECT THAT YOU WOULD *BELIEVE* ME.
Delicious Ice Cream Company
SOMETHING STINKS, MISS GONZALES. AND IT ISN'T WILD LILAC...

I AM BEING VERY FOOLISH.
HE WILL KILL ME FOR THIS-- JUST AS HE KILLED STEIN.

THIS IS STEELGRAVE'S PLACE.
IS HE IN THERE?
YES. AND MAVIS. HE WILL KILL HER, TOO.
LISTEN--

KISS ME, AMIGO, I HAVE NOT VERY LONG TO LIVE.

I pushed her away from me, but gently.

She lifted her right hand quickly.
There was a gun in it now.

I thought the gun would jump when she pulled the trigger. If I dropped at just the right moment—
— but I wasn't that good.

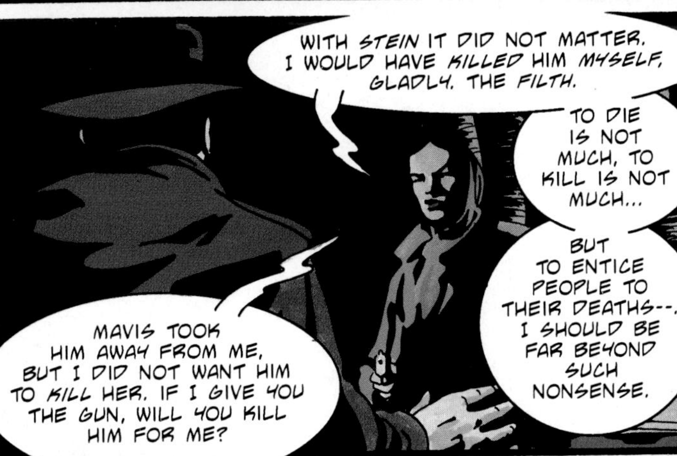
MAVIS TOOK HIM AWAY FROM ME, BUT I DID NOT WANT HIM TO KILL HER. IF I GIVE YOU THE GUN, WILL YOU KILL HIM FOR ME?
WITH STEIN IT DID NOT MATTER. I WOULD HAVE KILLED HIM MYSELF, GLADLY. THE FILTH.
TO DIE IS NOT MUCH, TO KILL IS NOT MUCH...
BUT TO ENTICE PEOPLE TO THEIR DEATHS--. I SHOULD BE FAR BEYOND SUCH NONSENSE.

I'D KILL HIM IF I HAD TO.

YOU THINK YOU ARE TOUGH, AMIGO. YOU ARE A VERY SOFT PEACH COMPARED WITH STEEL-GRAVE.
I HAVE KNOWN HIM A LONG TIME. I KNEW HIM IN CLEVELAND.

HE HAS KILLED A DOZEN MEN WITH A SMILE FOR EACH ONE.
WITH ICE PICKS?

GOOD NIGHT, AMIGO.

The car backed violently with a harsh tearing of the tires on the asphalt paving.
Then the lights drifted off among the trees and the sound faded into the long-drawn wheeze of tree frogs.
.32 caliber with a white bone grip.
Two less than a full load. It had been fired. Twice perhaps.
Orrin Quest had been shot twice. The two shells I picked up on the floor were .32 caliber.
And yesterday afternoon, in room 332 of the Hotel Van Nuys, a blond girl with a towel in front of her face...
...had pointed a .32 caliber automatic at me with a white bone grip.
You can get too fancy about these things.
You can also not get fancy enough...

I didn't think the door would be unlocked for my convenience, so I prowled around until I found a door under the wooden steps to the service entrance.
A set of stairs led to a hallway, and at last I came to what should be the living room.
I could just make out the usual paraphernalia of a living room, plus some long, shadowed tables that told me the boys downtown had been right about that gambling rap.
Tigers could be in the darkness watching me. Or guys with large guns.
Or nothing and nobody and too much imagination in the wrong place.
HELLO, ANYBODY HERE NEEDING A DETECTIVE?
HELLO YOURSELF...
...I THINK YOU CAME TOO LATE.
TOO LATE FOR WHAT?
TOO LATE TO BE SHOT.
SHUCKS. I'VE BEEN LOOKING FORWARD TO IT ALL EVENING.
MISS GONZALES BROUGHT ME.
SHE MAY HAVE STARTED OUT TO. BUT SHE CHANGED HER MIND.
I KNOW. SHE'LL BE DISAPPOINTED AS HELL. SHE PUT YOU ON THE SPOT--JUST AS SHE DID STEIN.

WHAT A WAY YOU HAVE WITH THE GIRLS. HOW THE HELL DO YOU DO IT?
IT CAN'T BE YOUR CLOTHES OR YOUR PERSONALITY OR YOUR MONEY. YOU DON'T *HAVE* ANY.

YEAH. YOU WERE BORN WITH A SILVER CADILLAC IN YOUR MOUTH. AND I COULD GUESS WHERE.
COULD YOU?
DIDN'T THINK IT WAS A VERY TIGHT SECRET, DID YOU?
WHERE'S STEELGRAVE?

HE *WAS* HERE.
MAY I HAVE A CIGARETTE?
THE OLD CIGARETTE STALL. BUT I CAN'T MAKE UP MY MIND WHETHER YOU'RE STALLING TO GIVE SOMEONE TIME TO GET HERE--OR TO GIVE SOMEBODY TIME TO GET FAR AWAY.
SO WHERE IS STEELGRAVE?

YOU OUGHT TO BE *GLAD* WHEREVER HE IS. HE HAD TO KILL YOU. OR *THOUGHT* HE HAD.
YOU WANTED ME HERE, DIDN'T YOU? WERE YOU THAT FOND OF HIM?
I MUST HAVE BEEN, ONCE.

IT SEEMS LIKE A THOUSAND YEARS AGO I MET A NICE QUIET GUY WHO KNEW HOW TO BEHAVE IN PUBLIC AND DIDN'T SHOOT HIS CHARM AROUND.

YES, I LIKED HIM. I LIKED HIM A LOT.
AND IN THE END I LIKED HIM WITH *THIS*.

Yes. That made two fired all around.

TRY THAT CHAIR BY THE WINDOW.

I went over there walking in low gear.

No blood moved in him and very little had stained his jacket.

I wiped my hands off on my handkerchief and stood for a little longer looking down at his quiet face.

The bullet had gone through the outside pocket of his double-breasted jacket.
It had been fired by someone who knew where the heart was.

WHAT DID YOU EXPECT ME TO DO? HE KILLED MY BROTHER.
SOMEBODY HAD TO--AND QUICK.
DIDN'T YOU EVER WONDER WHY STEELGRAVE NEVER WENT AFTER ME AND WHY HE LET YOU GO TO THE VAN NUYS YESTERDAY INSTEAD OF GOING HIMSELF?
DIDN'T YOU EVER WONDER WHY A FELLOW WITH HIS RESOURCES AND EXPERIENCE NEVER TRIED TO GET HOLD OF THOSE PHOTOGRAPHS, NO MATTER WHAT HE HAD TO DO TO GET THEM?

HOW LONG HAVE YOU KNOWN THE PHOTOGRAPHS EXISTED?

WEEKS, NEARLY TWO MONTHS. I GOT ONE IN THE MAIL A COUPLE OF DAYS AFTER--
AFTER STEIN WAS KILLED.
DID YOU THINK STEELGRAVE HAD KILLED STEIN?

NO. WHY SHOULD I?
UNTIL *TONIGHT*, THAT IS.

WHAT HAPPENED AFTER YOU GOT THE PHOTO?

MY BROTHER ORRIN CALLED ME UP AND SAID HE HAD LOST HIS JOB AND WAS BROKE. HE WANTED MONEY.
HE DIDN'T SAY ANYTHING ABOUT THE PHOTO. HE DIDN'T HAVE TO. THERE WAS ONLY ONE TIME IT COULD HAVE BEEN TAKEN.
THEN WHAT? MORE PRINTS OF THE PHOTO?
ONE EVERY WEEK.
I SHOWED THEM TO *HIM*.

HE DIDN'T LIKE IT.
I DIDN'T TELL HIM ABOUT ORRIN. I SUPPOSE HE MUST HAVE FOUND OUT.

BUT NOT WHERE ORRIN WAS HIDING OUT, OR HE WOULDN'T HAVE WAITED THIS LONG.
WHEN DID YOU TELL HIM?

I TOLD HIM TODAY.
PLEASE DON'T ASK ME A LOT OF USELESS QUESTIONS. THERE'S NOTHING YOU CAN DO. I *THOUGHT* THERE WAS--WHEN I CALLED DOLORES. THERE ISN'T NOW.

YOU'RE GOING TOO FAST FOR ME. YOU DIDN'T KNOW WHEN YOU WENT TO THE VAN NUYS THAT STEELGRAVE WAS WEEPY MOYER. SO WHAT DID YOU GO THERE FOR?
WHEN HE WAS IN JAIL THAT TIME, I HAD TO KNOW THERE WAS *SOMETHING* ABOUT HIM THAT HE DIDN'T CARE TO HAVE KNOWN.

I KNEW HE HAD BEEN IN SOME KIND OF RACKET, I GUESS.
BUT NOT *KILLING* PEOPLE.
ALL RIGHT. THERE'S SOMETHING YOU DON'T SEEM TO UNDERSTAND.
STEELGRAVE KNEW THAT SOONER OR LATER THE BLACKMAILER HAD TO SHOW HIMSELF. THAT WAS WHAT HE WAS WAITING FOR.

HE DIDN'T CARE ANYTHING ABOUT THE PHOTO ITSELF, EXCEPT FOR YOUR SAKE.
HE KILLED MY BROTHER.

YOU WERE FOND OF HIM ONCE.

I STOPPED BEING FOND OF HIM LAST NIGHT. HE SAW YOU LEAVING MY APARTMENT. HE ASKED ABOUT YOU, WHO YOU WERE AND SO ON.
I TOLD HIM.
I TOLD HIM I WOULD HAVE TO ADMIT THAT I WAS AT THE VAN NUYS HOTEL WHEN THAT MAN WAS LAYING THERE DEAD.

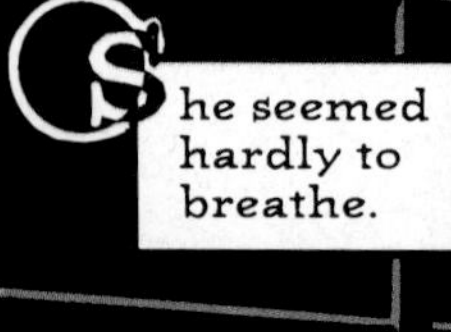

She seemed hardly to breathe.

Then she turned abruptly and walked away. I waited for her to look back.

She went on without turning.

CHATEAU BERCY? DOLORES GONZALES, PLEASE.
When she answered, I could almost hear her breath catch. Not quite. You can't really hear it over the phone. Sometimes you think you can.
She claimed that Steelgrave had tried to ditch the gun on her earlier that night. I told her to forget I had called, and went back to Steelgrave.
I took out the gun Dolores had given me and wiped it off and put his limp hand around the butt, held it there and let go.
The gun thudded to the carpet. The position looked natural.
That left me with three guns. There was a weapon in his holster that I took out and put under a counter wrapped in a towel. My luger I didn't touch. The other white-handled automatic was left.
I fired two shots that nicked peacefully into the wall.
I couldn't tell whether the big muscle on the side of his neck had begun to set or not. But his skin was colder that it had been.
There was not a hell of a lot of time to play around with.
YEAH, GET ME THE HOMICIDE BUREAU, DETECTIVE CHRISTY FRENCH...

They came in as they should, big, tough and quiet, their eyes flickering with watchfulness and cautious with disbelief.
POLICE

DEAD, WOULDN'T YOU SAY?
FINGER-PRINTS IN ALL THE RIGHT PLACES, I HOPE.
YOU HERE WHEN HE GOT IT, MARLOWE?
NO.
A GIRL I KNOW CALLED ME THIS EVENING AND SAID A CLIENT OF MINE WAS IN DANGER UP HERE-- FROM HIM. THIS GIRL RODE ME UP HERE.
SOMEBODY WITH A NAME?

DOLORES GONZALES, CHATEAU BERCY APARTMENTS. ON FRANKLIN.
SHE'S IN PICTURES.
OH-HO.

WHO'S YOUR CLIENT? SAME ONE?
NO. THIS IS ANOTHER PARTY ALTOGETHER.

HAVE A NAME?
NOT YET. THERE HAS TO BE SOME AGREEMENT ABOUT PUBLICITY.
THE D.A. OUGHT TO BE WILLING.

YOU DON'T KNOW THE D.A. GOOD, MARLOWE.
HE EATS PUBLICITY LIKE I EAT TENDER YOUNG GARDEN PEAS.
SHE HASN'T ANY NAME...

THERE ARE A DOZEN WAYS WE CAN FIND OUT, KID.
WHY GO INTO THIS ROUTINE THAT MAKES IT TOUGH FOR ALL OF US?

GODDAMN IT, THIS MAN KILLED ORRIN QUEST!
YOU TAKE THAT GUN DOWNTOWN AND CHECK IT AGAINST THE BULLETS IN QUEST! GIVE ME THAT MUCH, AT LEAST.

I WOULDN'T GIVE YOU THE DIRTY END OF A BURNT MATCH.

I WON'T LIE TO YOU. AND I WON'T TELL YOU ANYTHING EXCEPT ON THE TERMS I STATED.

PUT THE CUFFS ON HIM, FRED. BEHIND.
HE'S UNDER ARREST...

Ten hours and a pot of bitter black coffee later and I felt like the box of shavings the cat had had kittens in. They made me sit up in a chair all night, but in the end it was as tough a job as they ever didn't do.
The good doctor Lagardie had disappeared, but they did find out that I had been right on the Cleveland angle.
I hated it to be that tidy.
Orrin Quest wants to put the bite on Steelgrave. So he just by pure accident runs into the one guy in Bay City that can prove who Steelgrave was. But when that photo was taken Stein hadn't been squibbed off. SOMEBODY had to tell him.
In any event, it seemed to be a dead issue. Clausen and Mileaway Marsten both had records. Orrin Quest was dead, and the police weren't going to drag his family through the mud just to prove they could solve a case.

As for Steelgrave, an investigation doesn't last long when a gangster gets his.
There was no question of identity. Off the record, they had been sure that Steelgrave was Moyer all along, they just didn't have a thing on him.

And the guns both belonged to Steelgrave. One of them killed Quest. The same gun killed Stein.
DISTRICT ATTORNEY
It would be hell if the ballistics man got them mixed up.
YOU'RE IN A BAD SPOT, MARLOWE...

...YOU DON'T LOOK GOOD AT ALL.
YOU'VE BEEN CAUGHT SUPPRESSING EVIDENCE HELPFUL TO THE SOLUTIONS OF A MURDER. THAT IS OBSTRUCTING JUSTICE. YOU COULD GO UP FOR IT.

WHAT EVIDENCE?

JUST A MOMENT. IS THAT PHOTO THE EVIDENCE MISTER MARLOWE IS SUPPOSED TO HAVE SUP-PRESSED?
AS MISS WELD'S ATTORNEY, I'D HAVE TO POINT OUT THAT THAT PHOTO ISN'T EVIDENCE OF ANYTHING.
MISTER FARRELL, I'LL ASK THE QUESTIONS

MISS WELD, ARE YOU PREPARED TO TAKE THE STAND AND SWEAR AS TO THE TIME AND PLACE WHEN THIS PHOTOGRAPH WAS TAKEN?
NO, MISTER ENDICOTT, I COULDN'T. I DIDN'T KNOW IT WAS BEING TAKEN.

ALL YOU HAVE TO DO IS *LOOK* AT IT.

AND ALL I KNOW IS WHAT I *GET* FROM LOOKING AT IT.
I'VE HAD LOTS OF PHOTOS TAKEN OF ME, MISTER ENDICOTT. IN A LOT OF DIFFERENT PLACES AND WITH A LOT OF DIFFERENT PEOPLE.

I HAVE HAD LUNCH AND DINNER AT THE "DANCERS" WITH MISTER STEEL-GRAVE AND WITH VARIOUS OTHER MEN.
I DON'T KNOW WHAT YOU WANT ME TO SAY.

IF I UNDER-STAND YOUR POINT, YOU WOULD LIKE MISS WELD TO BE YOUR WITNESS--
--TO CONNECT THIS PHOTO UP.
IN WHAT KIND OF *PROCEEDING?*

THAT'S MY BUSINESS. SOMEBODY SHOT STEELGRAVE TO DEATH LAST NIGHT. IT COULD HAVE BEEN ANYBODY.
IT COULD HAVE EVEN BEEN MISS WELD.
I'M SORRY TO SAY THAT, BUT IT SEEMS TO BE IN THE CARDS.

WELL, LET'S ASSUME A PROCEEDING, ONE IN WHICH THAT PHOTO IS PART OF YOUR EVIDENCE--IF YOU CAN GET IT IN.
BUT YOU CAN'T. MISS WELD WON'T GET IT IN FOR YOU.

YOU'D HAVE TO CONNECT IT UP WITH A WITNESS WHO COULD SWEAR AS TO WHEN, HOW AND WHERE IT WAS TAKEN.
OTHERWISE I'D OBJECT--IF I HAPPENED TO BE ON THE OTHER SIDE.

THE ONLY MAN WHO COULD CONNECT IT UP IS THE MAN WHO TOOK IT. I UNDERSTAND HE'S DEAD.
THIS PHOTO IS CLEAR EVIDENCE IN AND OF ITSELF THAT AT A CERTAIN TIME AND PLACE STEELGRAVE WAS NOT IN JAIL, AND THEREFORE HAD NO ALIBI FOR THE KILLING OF STEIN.

IT'S EVIDENCE WHEN AND IF YOU GET IT INTRODUCED AS EVIDENCE, ENDICOTT.
FOR PETE'S SAKE, FORGET THAT PICTURE. IT PROVES NOTHING WHATSOEVER.
AND IF THAT'S THE EVIDENCE MARLOWE SUPPRESSED, THEN HE DIDN'T IN A LEGAL SENSE SUPPRESS EVIDENCE AT ALL.

I WASN'T THINKING OF TRYING STEELGRAVE FOR MURDER, BUT I AM A LITTLE INTERESTED IN WHO KILLED HIM.

ARE YOU SURE HE WAS MURDERED?
I UNDERSTAND TWO GUNS WERE FOUND, BOTH THE PROPERTY OF STEELGRAVE.

ONE OF THESE GUNS HAD KILLED QUEST AND ALSO STEIN. THE OTHER HAD KILLED STEELGRAVE. FIRED AT CLOSE QUARTERS, TOO.

I ADMIT THOSE BOYS DON'T AS A RULE TAKE THAT WAY OUT. BUT IT COULD HAPPEN.
NO DOUBT. THANKS FOR THE SUGGESTION. IT HAPPENS TO BE WRONG.

MISS WELD, THIS OFFICE DOESN'T BELIEVE IN SEEKING PUBLICITY AT THE EXPENSE OF PEOPLE TO WHOM IT MIGHT BE FATAL.
IT IS MY DUTY TO DETERMINE WHETHER ANYONE SHOULD BE BROUGHT TO TRIAL FOR ANY OF THESE MURDERS, AND TO PROSECUTE THEM.

I DON'T THINK YOU HAVE BEEN QUITE *CANDID* WITH ME ABOUT THIS PHOTOGRAPH, BUT I WON'T PRESS THE MATTER NOW.

THERE IS NOT MUCH POINT IN MY ASKING YOU WHETHER YOU SHOT STEELGRAVE.
BUT I DO ASK YOU WHETHER YOU HAVE ANY KNOWLEDGE THAT WOULD POINT TO WHO MAY OR MIGHT HAVE KILLED HIM.

KNOWLEDGE, MISS WELD--NOT MERE *SUSPICION.*

NO.

WELL.
THAT WILL BE ALL FOR NOW THEN.
MISS WELD, MISTER ENDICOTT. THANKS FOR COMING IN.

She didn't seem to look at me when she went out, but some-thing touched the back of my hand lightly.
Robinson leads Dodgers over Giants, 5-2

Probably accidental.
Her sleeve.

YOU'RE NOT EXACTLY PROUD OF THE WAY YOU'VE HANDLED THINGS, ARE YOU, MARLOWE?

I GOT OFF ON THE WRONG FOOT.
AFTER THAT I JUST HAD TO TAKE MY LUMPS.

I COULD MAKE A LOT OF ANSWERS TO THAT. THEY'D ALL SOUND ABOUT THE SAME.
THANKS FOR COMING IN...

I went back to the office and unlocked the door and sniffed the twice-breathed air and the smell of dust.
HELLO...
I was just talking to the office equipment, the three green filing cases, the threadbare piece of carpet, the customer's chairs across from me, and the light fixture in the ceiling with three dead moths in it that had been there for at least six months.
I was talking to the pebbled glass panel and the grimy woodwork and the tired, tired telephone.
I was talking to the scales of an alligator, the name of the alligator being Marlowe, a private detective in our thriving little community.
Not the brainiest guy in the world, but cheap.
He started out cheap and he ended cheaper still.
IT'S ME, MISTER MARLOWE...

Orfamay Quest.
...I'M GOING HOME.
She was right back where she started that first morning. Same square bag, same rimless glasses, same prim little narrow-minded smile.

BACK TO MANHATTAN. CAN YOU AFFORD IT?
I CAN'T REMEMBER WHETHER I GAVE YOU BACK YOUR TWENTY DOLLARS OR NOT.
OH, YOU GAVE IT TO ME.
I NEVER MAKE MISTAKES ABOUT MONEY.

I WISH YOU'D TELL ME WHAT HAPPENED TO ORRIN. I'M ALL CONFUSED.
I TOLD YOU HE PROBABLY WENT OFF THE RAILS.
ABNORMAL SORT OF HOME LIFE. VERY INHIBITED SORT OF GUY WITH A VERY HIGHLY DEVELOPED SENSE OF HIS OWN IMPORTANCE.

I DON'T WANT TO GO PSYCHOLOGICAL ON YOU, BUT I FIGURE HE WAS JUST THE TYPE TO GO VERY COMPLETELY HAYWIRE.

THEN THERE'S THAT AWFUL MONEY HUNGER THAT RUNS IN YOUR FAMILY--
--ALL EXCEPT ONE.

If she thought I meant her, that was Jake with me.

THERE'S JUST ONE QUESTION I WANT TO ASK YOU. WAS YOUR FATHER MARRIED BEFORE?
WHY, YES.
THAT HELPS. LEILA HAD ANOTHER MOTHER. THAT SUITS ME FINE.

TELL ME SOME MORE. AFTER ALL I DID A LOT OF WORK FOR YOU, FOR A VERY LOW FEE OF NO DOLLARS NET.
YOU GOT PAID. WELL PAID. BY LEILA.
AND DON'T EXPECT ME TO CALL HER MAVIS WELD. I WON'T DO IT.

YOU DIDN'T KNOW I WAS GOING TO GET PAID.

WELL...

...YOU DID GET PAID.

OKAY. PASS THAT.
HOW DID ORRIN FIND OUT SOMETHING ABOUT STEELGRAVE THAT THE COPS DIDN'T KNOW?

I--I DON'T KNOW.
COULD IT HAVE BEEN THAT DOCTOR?

OH SURE. HE AND ORRIN GOT TO BE FRIENDS SOMEHOW.
A COMMON INTEREST IN SHARP TOOLS MAYBE.

There was a tidy little silence while she looked at her bag again.
I was beginning to get curious about that bag.

WHY DID ORRIN CALL UP NIGHT BEFORE LAST?
HE WAS-- HE WAS *SCARED* DOCTOR LAGARDIE WASN'T *PLEASED* WITH HIM ANYMORE.
S-SOMETHING ABOUT SOME *PICTURES.* SOMEBODY HAD *TAKEN* THEM FROM HIM.
ORRIN DIDN'T KNOW WHO, BUT HE WAS *SCARED.*

I HAD THEM.
I STILL HAVE.

...I--I DON'T *BELIEVE* YOU.

I got up and opened the drawer. In a moment I was back with the envelope.
I poured the prints and the negative out on the desk — my side of the desk.

I'D LOVE TO SEE SOME OF THOSE LETTERS HE WROTE HOME. I BET THEY'RE MEATY.

I COULD *MAKE* YOU GIVE THE PICTURES TO THE *POLICE.*

YOU COULD TRY.
TELL ME, WHO TIPPED OFF THE POLICE THAT LAGARDIE KNEW CLAUSEN? LAGARDIE THOUGHT I DID. I DIDN'T. SO YOU DID.
WHY? SAME REASON YOU HIRED ME. TO SMOKE OUT YOUR BROTHER WHO WAS NOT CUTTING YOU IN--BECAUSE RIGHT THEN HE HAD LOST HIS DECK OF CARDS AND WAS HIDING OUT.

Y-YOU'RE FILTHY. YOU'RE VILE.
HOW DARE YOU SAY SUCH THINGS TO ME.

HOW MUCH DOUGH DID YOU SQUEEZE OUT OF THE DEAL?

YOU LEAVE MY BAG ALONE!

I pulled it in front of me and snapped it open.
There was nothing until I came to the zipper pocket at the back.

L-LEILA GAVE ME THE MONEY.
LEILA DIDN'T GIVE YOU THAT MONEY.

STEELGRAVE GAVE IT TO YOU. BECAUSE YOU KNEW WHERE ORRIN WAS.

YOUR OWN BROTHER. YOU SET HIM UP SO THEY COULD KILL HIM.

LEILA TOLD HIM. LEILA DID IT.

LEILA TOLD ME SHE TOLD HIM. BUT SHE'S NOT THE BLOOD MONEY TYPE.
A THOUSAND DOLLARS. I HOPE YOU'RE HAPPY WITH IT.

I COULD TELL THE *POLICE*. I COULD TELL THEM A LOT OF THINGS. THEY'D BELIEVE ME.

AND I COULD TELL THEM WHO SHOT STEEL-GRAVE.
THEY MIGHT BELIEVE *ME*.

WHO COULD *PROVE* IT? WHO'S *ALIVE* TO PROVE IT? *YOU*? WHO ARE YOU? A CHEAP SHYSTER, A NOBODY.
WHY, EVEN TWENTY DOLLARS BUYS YOU.

WHAT DO YOU EXPECT?
I DON'T HAVE ANY BROTHERS OR SISTERS TO SELL OUT.

She stopped dead, frozen in a kind of horror. The light glinted on her glasses.
There were no eyes behind them.
But I knew they were fixed on the little smoldering heap of prints in the ash tray.

Then the telephone rang and she jumped a foot.

I turned to answer it.
HELLO.
AMIGO, ARE YOU ALL RIGHT?

There was a sound in the background.

I swung around and saw the door click shut.

I'M TIRED. I'VE BEEN UP ALL NIGHT. APART FROM--
WOULD YOU LIKE TO TAKE ME TO LUNCH?
I MIGHT. ARE YOU HOME?

SÍ.
I'LL COME OVER IN A LITTLE WHILE.

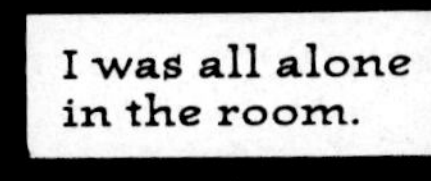
I was all alone in the room.

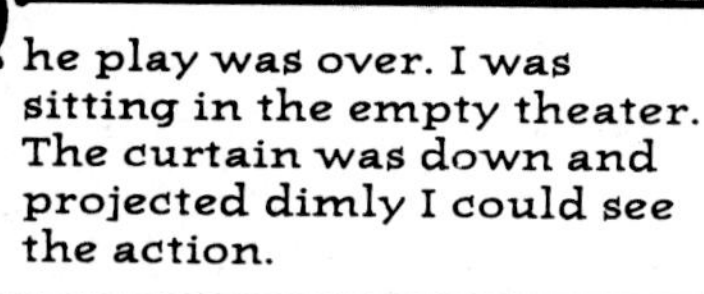

But already some of the actors were getting vague and unreal. The little sister above all. Because in a way she WAS so unreal.

I thought of her tripping back to Manhattan, Kansas, and old mom, with that fat little new thousand dollars in her purse. A few people had been killed so she could get it, but I didn't think that would bother her for long.

IT WAS JUST THAT IN THOSE DAYS IT WAS FUN TO KNOW A GANGSTER. ONE WENT TO THE PLACES WHERE THEY WERE SAID TO GO AND IF ONE WAS LUCKY, PERHAPS SOME EVENING--
WHAT ABOUT YOUR HUSBAND? OR DON'T YOU REMEMBER?
THE STREETS OF THE WORLD ARE PAVED WITH DISCARDED HUSBANDS.

ISN'T IT THE TRUTH? YOU FIND THEM EVERY-WHERE.
EVEN IN BAY CITY.
MIGHT EVEN BE A GRADUATE OF THE SORBONNE. MIGHT EVEN BE MOONING AWAY IN A MEASLY SMALL TOWN PRACTICE.

THAT'S A COINCIDENCE I'D LIKE TO EAT.
IT HAS A TOUCH OF POETRY, EH, AMIGO?

YOU DON'T USE MUCH SPANISH, DO YOU?
"AMIGO" GETS WORN TO SHREDS.

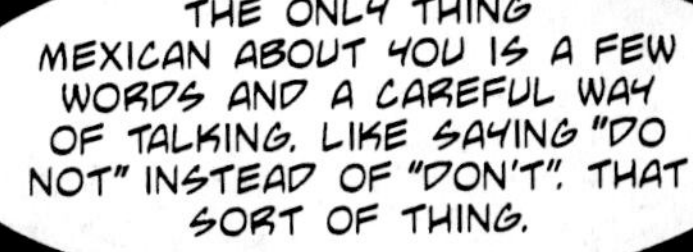

THE ONLY THING MEXICAN ABOUT YOU IS A FEW WORDS AND A CAREFUL WAY OF TALKING. LIKE SAYING "DO NOT" INSTEAD OF "DON'T". THAT SORT OF THING.

I'M IN BAD TROUBLE DOWNTOWN.
APPARENTLY MISS WELD HAD THE GOOD SENSE TO TELL HER BOSS AND HE CAME THROUGH. GOT LEE FARRELL FOR HER.
I DON'T THINK THEY THINK SHE SHOT STEELGRAVE. BUT THEY THINK I KNOW WHO DID, AND THEY DON'T LOVE ME ANYMORE.
AND DO YOU KNOW, AMIGO?

I TOLD ORFAMAY I DID.

...I WAS THERE, AMIGO...

"...IT WAS VERY CURIOUS, REALLY. THE LITTLE GIRL HAD BEEN STAYING HERE WITH ME. SHE WANTED TO SEE STEELGRAVE'S HOUSE. SHE HAD NEVER SEEN A GAMBLING HOUSE, SHE SAID.
"SO I CALLED HIM UP AND HE SAID COME ALONG.
"WHEN WE GOT THERE HE PUT HIS ARM AROUND LITTLE ORFAMAY AND TOLD HER SHE HAD EARNED HER MONEY WELL.
"HE SAID HE HAD SOMETHING FOR HER; THEN HE TOOK FROM HIS POCKET A CLOTH OF SOME KIND AND GAVE IT TO HER.

"WHEN SHE UNWRAPPED IT THERE WAS A HOLE IN THE MIDDLE OF IT AND THE HOLE WAS STAINED WITH BLOOD.
"LITTLE ORFAMAY TOOK THE CLOTH AND STARED AT IT AND THEN STARED AT HIM AND HER FACE WAS VERY STILL.
"THEN SHE THANKED HIM AND OPENED HER BAG TO PUT THE CLOTH IN IT, AS I THOUGHT--IT WAS ALL VERY CURIOUS--

"--BUT INSTEAD SHE TOOK A GUN OUT OF HER BAG.
"SHE TURNED AROUND AND SHOT HIM DEAD WITH ONE SHOT."

YOU MADE HER CONFESS TO MAVIS WELD. AND LAST NIGHT WHEN YOU RUSHED ME OUT THERE, YOU ALREADY KNEW HE WAS DEAD AND THERE WASN'T ANYTHING TO BE AFRAID OF AND ALL THAT ACT WITH THE GUN WAS JUST AN ACT.
MAVIS WAS *DETERMINED* TO TAKE THE *BLAME*.
I CHASED HER OUT. SHE TOLD ME SHE HAD SHOT HIM. SHE HAD THE GUN. THE TWIN OF THE ONE YOU GAVE ME. YOU PROBABLY DIDN'T NOTICE YOURS HAD BEEN FIRED.
I KNOW *VERY LITTLE* ABOUT GUNS.

SURE. I COUNTED THE SHELLS IN IT. TWO HAD BEEN FIRED.
QUEST WAS KILLED WITH TWO SHOTS FROM A .32 AUTOMATIC. SAME CALIBER. I PICKED UP THE SHELLS IN THE DEN DOWN THERE.

DOWN WHERE, AMIGO?

OF COURSE I COULDN'T KNOW IT WAS THE SAME GUN...
...BUT IT SEEMED WORTH TRYING OUT. ONLY CONFUSE THINGS UP A LITTLE, ANYHOW, AND GIVE MAVIS THAT MUCH OF A BREAK.

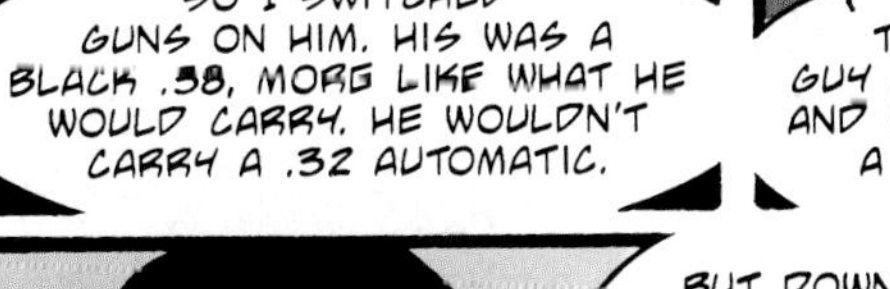
SO I SWITCHED GUNS ON HIM. HIS WAS A BLACK .38, MORE LIKE WHAT HE WOULD CARRY. HE WOULDN'T CARRY A .32 AUTOMATIC.

AND IF HE KILLED A MAN HE WOULD KILL HIM DEAD, AND BE SURE OF IT.
THIS GUY GOT UP AND WALKED A BIT.
WHICH GUY? I AM AFRAID I AM NOT *FOLLOWING* YOU TOO WELL.

I'D LIKE TO SAY HE TALKED A BIT. BUT HE DIDN'T.
HIS LUNGS WERE FULL OF BLOOD. HE DIED AT MY FEET.
DOWN THERE.

BUT DOWN *WHERE?* YOU HAVE NOT TOLD ME WHERE IT WAS THAT THIS--

DO I HAVE TO? YOU WERE PRESENT WHEN LITTLE ORFAMAY TOLD HIM WHERE TO GO. ONLY HE DIDN'T GO.
THAT'S WHAT'S BEEN THE MATTER ALL ALONG. I JUST WOULDN'T BUY WHAT WAS STARING ME IN THE FACE.

STEEL-GRAVE WAS A REFORMED CHARACTER AND DOING FINE.
THEN THIS STEIN COMES BOTHERING HIM, WANTING TO CUT IN. HE HAS TO GO. STEELGRAVE DOESN'T WANT TO KILL ANYBODY, BUT HE HAS TO GET RID OF STEIN.
SO HE GETS HIMSELF PINCHED. AND HE GETS OUT OF JAIL BY BRIBING THE JAIL DOCTOR, AND HE KILLS STEIN AND GOES BACK INTO JAIL AT ONCE.

WHEN THE KILLING SHOWS UP WHOEVER LET HIM OUT OF JAIL IS GOING TO RUN LIKE HELL BECAUSE THE COPS WILL COME OVER AND ASK QUESTIONS.
VERY NATURALLY, AMIGO.
SO FAR SO GOOD. BUT WHY DID HE LET THEM HOLD HIM FOR TEN DAYS?

ANSWER ONE, TO MAKE HIMSELF AN ALIBI.
ANSWER TWO, BECAUSE HE KNEW THAT SOONER OR LATER--
--THIS QUESTION OF HIM BEING MOYER WAS GOING TO GET AIRED, SO WHY NOT GIVE THEM THE TIME AND GET IT OVER WITH?

YOU LIKE THAT IDEA, AMIGO?

YES. BUT LOOK AT IT THIS WAY.
WHY WOULD HE HAVE LUNCH IN A PUBLIC PLACE ON THE VERY DAY HE WAS OUT OF THE COOLER TO KNOCK STEIN OFF?

AND IF HE DID, WHY WOULD YOUNG QUEST HAPPEN AROUND TO SNAP THAT PICTURE?
STEIN HADN'T BEEN KILLED YET.
I LIKE PEOPLE TO BE LUCKY, BUT THAT'S TOO LUCKY.

AGAIN, EVEN IF STEELGRAVE DIDN'T KNOW HIS PICTURE HAD BEEN TAKEN, HE KNEW WHO QUEST WAS. MUST HAVE.
HE WAS MAVIS WELD'S BOYFRIEND. HE MUST HAVE KNOWN SOMETHING OF THIS BROTHER OF HERS.

WHICH SIMPLY ADDS UP TO THE RESULT THAT THAT NIGHT OF ALL NIGHTS STEELGRAVE WOULD NOT HAVE SHOT STEIN--EVEN IF HE HAD PLANNED TO.

IT IS NOW FOR ME TO ASK YOU WHO DID.

"SOMEBODY WHO KNEW STEIN AND COULD GET CLOSE TO HIM.
"SOMEBODY WHO ALREADY KNEW THAT PHOTO HAD BEEN TAKEN, KNEW WHO STEELGRAVE WAS, KNEW THAT MAVIS WELD WAS ON THE VERGE OF BECOMING A BIG STAR, KNEW THAT HER ASSOCIATION WITH STEELGRAVE WAS DANGEROUS.

"SOMEBODY WHO HAD MET QUEST AT MAVIS WELD'S APARTMENT AND HAD GIVEN HIM THE WORKS, AND HE WAS A BOY THAT COULD BE KNOCKED CLEAN OUT OF HIS MIND BY THAT SORT OF TREATMENT.
LAKE · PRESTON
BOGART

"SOMEBODY WHO KNEW THOSE BONE-HANDLED .32'S WERE REGISTERED TO STEELGRAVE....

"...ALTHOUGH HE HAD ONLY BOUGHT THEM TO GIVE TO A COUPLE OF GIRLS.

"SOMEBODY WHO--"
"STOP!"

YOU WILL STOP AT ONCE, PLEASE! I WILL NOT TOLERATE THIS ANOTHER MINUTE. YOU WILL GO NOW!

WHY DID YOU KILL QUEST?

FOR TWO REASONS, AMIGO. HE WAS MORE THAN A LITTLE CRAZY AND IN THE END HE WOULD HAVE KILLED ME.
AND THE OTHER REASON IS THAT NONE OF THIS--ABSOLUTELY NONE OF IT--WAS FOR MONEY.
IT WAS FOR LOVE.

NO MATTER HOW MANY LOVERS A PERSON MAY HAVE, THERE IS ALWAYS ONE THAT YOU CANNOT BEAR TO LOSE TO ANOTHER.
STEELGRAVE WAS THE ONE.

THAT MAN I WOULD NOT SHARE.
I KILLED HIM.

AND YOU CANNOT DO A DAMN THING ABOUT ALL THIS, DARLING, UNLESS YOU DESTROY MAVIS WELD UTTERLY.
LAST NIGHT SHE PROVED THAT SHE WAS WILLING TO DESTROY HERSELF.

IF SHE WAS NOT ACTING.

THAT HURT, DID IT NOT? YOU ARE IN LOVE WITH HER.

THAT WOULD BE KIND OF SILLY.

I COULD SIT IN THE DARK WITH HER AND HOLD HANDS, BUT FOR HOW LONG?
IN A LITTLE WHILE SHE'D DRIFT OFF INTO A HAZE OF GLAMOUR AND EXPENSIVE CLOTHES.
SHE WON'T BE A REAL PERSON ANYMORE.

I'D WANT MORE THAN THAT.

QUERIDO-- I HAVE LIKED YOU VERY MUCH.
IT IS TOO BAD...

As I walked down the hall I didn't really expect a slug in the back. I thought she liked better having me the way I was—and not being able to do a damn thing about it.
She was one for the books all right.
Utterly beyond the moral laws of this or any world I could imagine.

The lobby of the Chateau Bercy was old but made over.
As the elevator opened a man stood there waiting for it.

...Dr. Lagardie...

CALL THE POLICE...!

They came fast—but not fast enough.
When they cracked the door, Doctor Lagardie was sitting on the couch, holding her pressed against his heart. His eyes were blind and there was bloody foam on his lips. He had bitten through his tongue.
Under her left breast lay the silver handle of a knife I had seen before. The handle was in the shape of a naked woman.
Perhaps I ought to have stopped him. Perhaps I had a hunch what he would do, and deliberately let him do it. Sometimes when I'm low I try to reason it out. But it gets too complicated. The whole damn case was that way. There was never a point where I could do the natural obvious thing without stopping to rack my head dizzy with figuring how it would affect somebody I owed something to.
The eyes of Miss Dolores Gonzales were half open and on her lips there was the dim ghost of a provocative smile. "The Hippocrates Smile," the ambulance intern said, and sighed.
He bent over and closed her eyes. "I guess somebody lost a dream."
END

RAP SHEET

Michael Lark, a talented young newcomer, first gained notice for his *AIRWAVES* and *TAKEN UNDER* series, published by Caliber Press, on which he collaborated with Debra Rodia. He also collaborated with P. Craig Russell on an adaptation of Ray Bradbury's *"The Visitor"* for *RAY BRADBURY COMICS*, published by Topps Comics. His work has appeared in the anthology *WEIRD BUSINESS* and *SHADE , THE CHANGING MAN*. Currently he is adapting two stories by Ambrose Bierce and illustrating Dean Motter's *TERMINAL CITY* for DC /Vertigo.

James Steranko's career is difficult to summarize in a few sentences. He was born in 1938, a few days after Orson Welles's famous *War of the Worlds* radio broadcast. Following a remarkable career as an escape artist and magician, he rocked the comic-book world with his innovative work on Marvel's *NICK FURY, AGENT OF S.H.I.E.L.D.* He continued trailblazing the medium with his work on *CAPTAIN AMERICA* and *THE X-MEN*. He has painted numerous paperback covers, including the memorable series of *SHADOW* covers. In 1970, he wrote and illustrated his homage to the world of *noir* fiction with the graphic novel *CHANDLER*, a character named in honor of Marlowe's creator. In addition to his continuing publishing efforts on Supergraphics' *PREVUE*, he has worked on various motion pictures including producing visualizations for Steven Spielberg's *Raiders of the Lost Ark* and collaborating with Francis Ford Coppola on *Bram Stoker's Dracula*.